$16 $^{99}$ new!

# THE
# SPEED
# CHRONICLES

# THE
# SPEED
# CHRONICLES

EDITED BY **JOSEPH MATTSON**

Published by Akashic Books
©2011 Akashic Books
Printed in Canada

ISBN-13: 978-1-61775-028-1
Library of Congress Control Number: 2011923103

Akashic Books
PO Box 1456
New York, NY 10009
info@akashicbooks.com
www.akashicbooks.com

*This book is dedicated to the liver—*
*the vital organ and the daring spirit*

# TABLE OF CONTENTS

*It shines in Paradise. It burns in Hell.*
—Gaston Bachelard, *The Psychoanalysis of Fire*


*I started hearing whispers from the people in the bedspread and in
the window glass, and though I was a little embarrassed at first, I
answered them, thinking, why deny anything?*
—William S. Burroughs, Jr., *Speed*


*The Bible never said anything about amphetamines.*
—"Fast" Eddie Felson in *The Color of Money*

# introduction
# some gods, some panthers
## by joseph mattson

**B**ecause some gods made work, ennui, depression, deadlines, and pain, and some gods (perhaps the selfsame mothers) made adventure, rapture, elation, creativity, and orgasm—and especially because some gods made dopamine—some gods made speed. The answer to some deserts is some jungles. While some panthers skulk breathily to rest after the hunt, some panthers hide out in the bush mad to live, licking their chops along with their wounds, transforming lovely day into lustful night, and they do speed.

*Speed*: the most demonized—and misunderstood—drug in the land. Deprived of the ingrained romantic mysticism of the opiate or the cosmopolitan chic of cocaine or the commonplace tolerance of marijuana, there is no sympathy for this devil. Yet speed—amphetamines (Dexedrine, Benzedrine, Adderall) and especially methamphetamine[*]; crystal, crank, ice, chickenscratch, Nazi dope, OBLIVION marching powder, the *go fast*—is the most American of drugs: twice the productivity at half the cost, and equal opportunity for all. It *feels* so good and *hurts* so bad. From its dueling roots of pharmacological miracle cure and Californian biker gang scourge to contemporary Ivy League campuses and high school chem labs, punk rock clubs

[*]Though MDMA/Ecstasy is chemically part of the amphetamine family, it has a singular place in the world and deserves a collection of its own (the forthcoming *The Ecstasy Chronicles*) and is not covered in the following stories. Conversely, Provigil (modafinil), while not structurally a part of the amphetamine family, is included for its eerily similar functionality to pharmaceutical amphetamines—new speed that works in part like old speed, and neoteric enough to find a home here.

to the military industrial complex, suburban households to tin-can ghettos, it crosses all ethnicities, genders, and geographies—from immigrants and heartlanders punching double factory shifts to clandestine border warlords undermining the DEA, doctors to bomber pilots, prostitutes to housewives, T-girls to teenagers, Academy Award–nominated actors to the poorest Indian on the rez—making it not only the most essentially American narcotic, but the most deceivingly sundry literary matter.

Some shoot for angst-curing kicks, some snort for sad endurance, some for explosive joyrides into the unknown, because no matter how delicious dying young might seem, they want to live forever.

The subject of speed is so innately intimidating yet so undeniably present that it begs to be written about. It is no secret that the drug has historically tuned up the lives of writers, including Jack Kerouac, Susan Sontag, Philip K. Dick, and scores more. Too rarely, though, has it been written of, and as California and the West, the Pacific Northwest, and now the Midwest, the South, and the East Coast toss for the crown of Speed Capital, U.S.A., its jolt to the bones of the American landscape continues to peak as it creeps onward into the farthest nooks of our physiography and consciousness. Wherever there is either something *or* nothing to do—wherever there is need for more gasoline on the fire—there is speed.

The majority of you, dear readers, have likely seen before-and-after anti-meth photo campaigns and have been at least brushed if not inundated with depictions of the horrors of the Crystal Death, but speed, like all sources of addiction, whether any of the brethren narcotics or food, sex, consumerism, and otherwise, is initially a wellspring for bliss. There are *reasons* people are willing to put the residue of acetone, lithium batteries, the red phosphorus of match heads, and other inorganic and toxic compounds the liver is not sure what to do with into their bodies: *It feels good. You get results.* The ancient longing to inhabit supernatural powers and kiss the orbits of gods is realized. The panther becomes superpanther with the rifle of a medicine cabinet. Anything is possible (giving credence to the old slogan, *Speed Kills*—rarely is ingesting speed a mortal wound; respectively, more people die or equally damage themselves from the feral, madcap things they do *on* speed than from the toxicity of the drug itself—except, of course, the lifers). Yes, it gets ugly, so ugly. But before your sex organs revert to embryonic acorns and your teeth fall out and feasting on your malnutrition are insects for your eyes only, it's a rush of pure euphoria and a seeming godsend to surmount all of life's daily tribulations.

Some panthers' antiphon to some gods' will.

Because speed is first and foremost an amplifier, the sparking ebullience and potential wretchedness it projects are possibilities already seeded in the human order, just waiting for the right drop of dew and hit of sunshine to come along and juice it up.

The fourteen stories in this book reflect not only both ends of the dichotomy above, but, more crucially, the abstractions within and between. Merely demonizing the drug would be the same crime as simply celebrating it. Condemning it outright and defending all recreational use are equal failures against illuminating the drug's complexity. The panther worships the god in a kaleidoscopic mayhem of alchemical felicity, and in real sorrow too. Though you'll find exultation and condemnation interwoven, these are no stereotypical tales of tweakers—the element of crime and the bleary-eyed zombies that have gone too far are here right alongside heart-wrenching narratives of everyday people, good intentions gone terribly awry, the skewed American Dream going up in flames, and even some accounts of unexpected joy. Juxtaposed with cir-

cumstances inherent to the drug (trying to score, the sheer veloc-
ity of uptake, the agony of withdrawal, death, etc.) are nuances
often elusive but central to speed's mores: camaraderie, compas-
sion, and charm.

Together with Scott Phillips's tale of Frank Sinatra's mummified penis as leverage in a surreptitious bulk cold medicine
deal and Kenji Jasper's meth murder-run by way of Capitol
Hill, you'll find Megan Abbott's benevolent doctor injecting
fast relief into disenchanted townsfolk and Jess Walter's bumbling
brothers-in-arms too innocuous for high crime. With Jerry Stahl's
no-punches-pulled, I mean *the* de facto nightmare scenarios
through amphetamine hell, and my own rendering of Hollywood
psychosis (the district in Los Angeles and, in part, its Tinseltown
abstract) gone to fanatics and sacrificial death-dogs, you'll find
William T. Vollmann's empathetic transsexual portrait of meth
as vitamin supplement and Beth Lisick's suburban housewife's giddy eagerness for validity and subsequent triumph.
There's James Franco's metafictional take on the cautionary
tale and Rose Bunch's story of Ozark yard wars together with
Tao Lin's disaffected New York City hipsters quietly pander-
ing for significance and Natalie Diaz's haunting embrace of
a sibling addict; Sherman Alexie's meth-induced war dancer
razing everything in his path, and James Greer's investigation of
the existential magical realism inherent in eliminating sleep from
one's diet.

I thank the authors—gods some, panthers some, and titans
all—for their incredible contributions. The dream roster has
come to fruition, and I remain ever humbled and appreciative
of their interest, generosity, trust, and guts to tango with the
beast.

Because some gods have ridden the rails, some panthers rail
the ride, 'scripts and spoons and straws raised like torches to

Rome. Let us now go unto stories of them and those whose lives they touch—let's go fast.

*Joseph Mattson*
*Los Angeles*
*September 2011*

# PART I
## MADNESS

NATALIE DIAZ was born and raised in the Fort Mojave Indian Village in Needles, California. She is Mojave and Pima. After playing professional basketball in Europe and Asia, she completed her MFA degree at Old Dominion University. She lives in Mohave Valley, Arizona, and directs a language revitalization program, working to document the few remaining Elder Mojave speakers. Her poetry and fiction has been published in the *Iowa Review, Bellingham Review, Prairie Schooner, Crab Orchard Review, Narrative, North American Review, Nimrod,* and others. Her first poetry book is forthcoming from Copper Canyon Press.

# how to go to dinner with a brother on drugs
## by natalie diaz

If he is wearing knives for eyes, if he has dressed for a Day of the Dead parade—three-piece skeleton suit, cummerbund of ribs—his pelvic girdle will look like a Halloween mask.

"The bones," he'll complain, make him itch. "Each ulna a tickle." His mandible might tingle.

He cannot stop scratching, so suggest that he change, but not because he itches—do it for the scratching. Do it for the bones.

"Okay, okay," he'll give in, "I'll change." He will return to his room, and as he climbs each stair, his back will be something else—one shoulder blade a failed wing, the other a silver shovel. He has not eaten in months. He will never change.

Still, you are happy he didn't come down with a headdress of green quetzal feathers, iridescent plumes dancing like an emerald blaze from his forehead, and a jaguar-pelt loincloth littered with mouth-shaped rosettes—because this beautiful drug usually dresses him up like a greed god, and tonight you are not in the mood to have your heart ripped out. Like the bloody-finger trick your father constructed for you and your brothers and sisters every Halloween—cut a hole in a small cardboard jewelry gift box, hold it in the palm of your hand, stick your middle finger up through the hole, pack gauze inside the box around your middle finger, cover the gauze and your finger in ketchup, shake a handful of dirt onto your finger, and then hold it up, your bloody-ketchup finger, to every person you see, explaining that you found it out in the road—it has gotten old, having your heart ripped out, being opened up that way.

He comes back down, this time dressed as a Judas effigy. "I know, I know," he'll joke, "It's not Easter. So what?"

Be straight with him. Tell him the truth. Tell him, "Judas had a rope around his neck."

When he asks if an old lamp cord will do, just shrug. He will go back upstairs, and you will be there, close enough to the door to leave, but you will not. You will wait, unsure of what you are waiting for. While you wait, go to the living room of your parents' home-turned-misery-museum. Explore the perpetual exhibits—"Someone Is Tapping My Phone," "*Como Deshacer a Tus Padres*," "*Mon Frère*"—ten, twenty, forty dismantled phones displayed on the dining table, red and blue wires snaking in and out, glinting snarls of copper, yellow computer chips, soft sheets of numbered rubber buttons, small magnets, jagged, ruptured shafts of lithium batteries, shells of Ataris, radios, and television sets cracked open like dark nuts, innards heaped across the floor. And by far the most beautiful, "Why Dad Can't Find the Lightbulbs"—a hundred glowing white bells of gutted lightbulbs, each rocking in a semicircle on the counter beneath your mom's hanging philodendron.

Your parents' home will look like an Al Qaeda yard sale. It will look like a bomb factory, which might give you hope, but you ought to know better than to hope. You are not so lucky—there is no fuse for you to find. For you and your family, there will be no quick ticket to Getaway Kingdom.

Think, all of this glorious mess could have been yours—not long ago, your brother lived with you. What was it you called it? "One last shot," a three-quarter-court heave, a buzzer-beater to win something of him back. But who were you kidding? You took him into your home with no naïve hopes of saving him, but instead to ease the guilt of never having tried.

He spent every evening in your bathroom with a turquoise BernzOmatic handheld propane torch, a meth-made Merlin mixing magic, chanting, "I will show you fear in a handful of dust," then shape-shifting into lions and tigers and bears and pacing your balcony, licking the air at your neighbors' wives and teenage daughters, fighting with the Hare in the Moon, conquering the night with his blue flame, and plotting to steal your truck keys, which you kept under your pillow.

Finally, you worked up the nerve to ask him to leave. He took his propane torch and left you with a Glad trash bag of filthy clothes and a meth pipe clanking in the dryer. Two weeks after that, God told him to do several things that got him arrested.

But since he is fresh-released from prison and living in your parents' home, you will be there to take him to dinner—because he is your brother, because you heard he was cleaning up. Mostly because you think you can handle dinner, a thing with a clear beginning and end, a specified amount of time, a ritual that everyone knows, even your brother. Sit down. Eat. Get up. Go home. You are optimistic about this well-now-that's-done-and-I'm-glad-it's-over kind of night.

If your brother doesn't come back down right away, if he takes his time, remember how long it took for the Minotaur to escape the labyrinth, and go to the sliding-glass window looking out onto the backyard. This is the exhibit whose fee is always too high, the reason you do not come to this place: your parents.

Your father will be out there, on the other side of the glass, wearing his *luchador* mask. He is *El Santo*. His face is pale. His face is bone white. His eyes are hollow teardrops. His mouth is a dark "Oh." He has worn it for years, still surprised by his life.

Do not even think of unmasking your father. That mask is the only fight he has left in him. He is all out of *planchas* and *topes*. He has no more *huracanranas* to give. Besides, *si tuvieras una máscara*, you would wear it.

Your father, *El Santo*, will pile mesquite logs into a pyre. Your mother will be out there too—wearing her sad dress made of flames—practicing lying on top of the pyre.

"It needs to be higher," she'll complain, "I've earned it."

See the single tower of hyacinth she clutches to her breast as she whispers to the violet petals, "*Ai, ai,* don't cry. *No hay mal que dure cien años.*" But the hyacinth will already have gone to ash, and knowing she is talking to herself, your throat will sting.

Your father will answer her as always, "Oh," which means he is imagining himself jumping over a top rope, out of the ring, running off, his silver-masked head cutting the night like a butcher knife.

Do not bother pounding against the glass. They will not look up. They know they cannot answer your questions.

Your brother will eventually make his way down to the front door. The lamp cord knotted at his neck should do the trick, so head to the restaurant.


In the truck, avoid looking at your brother dressed as a Judas effigy, but do not forget that a single match could devour him like a neon tooth, canopying him in a bright tent of pain—press the truck lighter into the socket.

The route will take you by a destroyed field—only months before, that earth was an explosion of cotton hulls—your headlights will slice across what remains of the wasted land, illuminating bleached clods of dirt and leftover cotton snagged here and there on a few wrecked stalks. The only despair greater than this field will be sitting next to you in the truck—his eyes are dark but loud and electric, like a cloud of locusts conducting a symphony of teeth. Meth—his singing siren, his jealous jinni conjuring up sandstorms within him, his harpy harem—has sucked the beauty from his face. He is a Cheshire Cat. His new face all jaw, all smile and bite.

Look at your brother. He is Borges's bestiary. He is a zoo of imaginary beings.

When he turns on the radio, "Fire" or "Manic Depression" will boom out. He will be your personal Jimi Hendrix. No, he will be your personal Geronimo playing air drums for Jimi Hendrix—large brown hands swooping and fluttering in rhythm against the dashboard like bats trapped in the cab of your truck, black hair whipping in the open window, tangling at the ends and sticking to the corners of his wide-open mouth shiny as a freshly dug hole, wet teeth flashing in the rearview mirror as he bobs his head to the beat.

Sigh. He is not Geronimo. Geronimo held out much longer. Your brother has clearly given up.

The sun is bound to lose its grip on the horizon, and when it does, the sky will burn red. It will be something you understand.

Search the road for something dead—to remind you that he is still alive, that you are ungrateful—a skunk whose head is matted to the faded asphalt, intestines ballooning from a quick strip of black and white like a strange carmine bloom.

"This is what it's like," you'll say aloud, "to be splayed open," but you will mean, *This is what it's like to rest.*

He will not hear you over the war party circling his skull—horses, hooves, drums, and whooping. "*Ai, ai, ai.*" He will smell the skunk and say, "Smells like *carne asada.*"

Your brother's jaw will become a third passenger in your truck—it will flex in the wind, resetting and rehinging, opening and closing against his will. It will occur to you that your brother is a beat-down, dubbed Bruce Lee—his words do not match his mouth, which is moving faster and faster. He is the fastest brother alive.

The next thing you'll know, you and your brother will be on Han's island, trapped in a steel chamber—being there with him, being there together, in that impossible cage, makes you root for him, makes you understand that you could lose him at any moment, so you love him.

When you were ten, your brother took you to the pow-wow down the street. He held your hand as you walked up to the open tailgates of the pickup-truck vendors and bought you and him each a pair of black wooden nunchucks with gold and green dragons up the sides. Bruce Lee was his hero. Back then, your brother was *Fists of Fury*. He was *Enter the Dragon*. He was *Game of Death I* and *II*. But back then was a long time ago. Now is now, and now you are here with a brother faster than Bruce Lee. Bruce Lee is dead. In a way, so is your brother. But you cannot forget how hard he practiced that summer. How he took his shirt off and acted out each scene in front of the bathroom mirror—touching his imaginary bloody lip with his fingertips, then tasting that imaginary blood, and making that "Wahhhh" Bruce Lee face as he swung his nunchucks over and under his shoulders. Remember the welts across his lower back and ribs? Remember how he cried when he hit himself in the chin?

Admit it—that was another brother. This brother is not Bruce Lee. This brother is Han. He is Han's steel chamber. Keep an eye on him—be prepared if he unscrews a metal hand at the wrist and replaces it with a metal bear claw. It would not shock you. He has done worse things. Face it. You are not here with him. You are here because of him. Do not be ashamed when it crosses your mind that you could end him quickly with a one-inch punch.

Your brother's lips are ruined. There is a sore in the right corner of his mouth. His teeth hurt, he says, his "dead mountain of carious teeth that cannot spit."

At the stop light, he will force you to look into his mouth. You hate his mouth. It is Švankmajer's rabbit hole—a bucket you've tripped over and fallen into for the last ten years. One of his teeth is cracked. He will want to go to the IHS dentist. "My teeth are falling out," he'll say, handing you a pointy incisor, telling you to put it under your pillow with your truck keys. When he says, "Make a wish," you will.

When you open your eyes, the light will be green, and he will still be there in front of you. His tooth will end up in the ashtray.

On the way there, he will wave to all the disheveled people walking along and across the roads—an itchy parade of twisting arms and legs pushing ratty strollers with big-headed, alien-eyed babies dangling rotten milk bottles over the stroller sides, a marching band of cheap cigarettes and dirty men and women disguised as an Exodus of rough-skinned Joshua trees, whose grinning mouths erupt in clouds of brown yucca moths that tick and splatter against your windshield.

Take a deep breath. You will be there soon.

Pull into the restaurant parking lot. Your brother will not want to wear his shoes inside. "Judas was barefoot," he will tell you.

"Judas wore sandals," you answer.

"No, Jesus wore sandals," he'll argue.

Not in that moment, but later, you will manage to laugh at the idea of arguing with a meth-head dressed like a Judas effigy about Jesus wearing sandals.

Night will be full-blown by the time you enter the restaurant—stars showing through like shotgun spread. Search your torso for a wound, a brother-shaped bullet hole pulsing like a Jesus side wound beneath your shirt. Even if you don't find it, remember that there are larger injuries than your own—your optimistic siblings, all white-haired and doubled over their beds, lost in great waves of prayer, sloshing in the belly of a dark whale named Monstruo, for this man who is half–wooden boy half-jackass.

Your brother will still itch when you are seated at your table. He will rake his fork against his skin. If you look closely, you will see that his skin is a desert—half a red racer is writhing in the middle of the long road of his forearm, a migration of tarantulas moves like a shadow across his sunken cheek.

Slide your fork and knife from the table. Hold them in your lap.

He will set his hands on the table—two mutts sleeping near the salsa, twitching with dreams of undressing cats.

He will lick his shattered lips at the waitress every time she walks by. He will tell you, then her, that he can taste her. If you are lucky, she will ignore him.

Pretend not to hear what he says. Also, ignore the cock crowing inside him, but if he notices that you notice, "Don't worry," he'll assure you, "the dogs will get it."

"Which dogs?" you have to ask.

Your brother will point out the window at two dogs humping in an empty lot across the way—slick pink tongues rolling and unrolling, hips jerking and trembling. Go ahead. Look closer, then clarify to your brother, "Those are not dogs. Those are *chupacabras*."

"*Chupacabras* are not real," he'll tell you, "brothers are."

The reflection in your empty plate will speak: "Your brother is on drugs. You are at a dinner that neither of you can eat."

Consider your brother. He is dressed as a Judas effigy admiring a pair of fuck-sick *chupacabras*—one dragging the other across the parking lot.

The waitress will come to take your order. Your brother will ask for a beer. You will pour your thirty pieces of silver onto the table and ask, "What can I get for this?"

**SHERMAN ALEXIE** is the best-selling author of *War Dances,* winner of the PEN/Faulkner Award for Fiction. He is also the author of *Reservation Blues, Indian Killer, The Toughest Indian in the World, Ten Little Indians, Flight, The Lone Ranger and Tonto Fistfight in Heaven, The Business of Fancy-dancing,* and *The Absolutely True Diary of a Part-Time Indian,* winner of the National Book Award for Young People's Literature. Also a filmmaker, stand-up comic, and public speaker, Alexie lives in Seattle, WA, with his wife and two sons.

# war cry
## by sherman alexie

Forget crack, my cousin said, meth is the new war dancer.
World champion, he said.

Grand Entry, he said.

Five bucks, he said, give me five bucks and I'll give you
enough meth to put you on a Vision Quest.

For a half-assed Indian, he sure talked full-on spiritual. He
was a born-again Indian. At the age of twenty-five, he war danced
for the first time. Around the same day he started dealing drugs.

I'm traditional, he said.

Rule is: whenever an Indian says he's traditional, you know
that Indian is full of shit.

But not long after my cousin started dancing, the powwow
committee chose him as Head Man Dancer. Meaning: he was
charming and popular. Powwow is like high school, except with
more feathers and beads.

He took drugs too, so he was doomed. But what Indian isn't
doomed? Anyway, the speed made him dance for hours. Little
fucker did somersaults. I've seen maybe three somersaulting war
dancers in my own life.

You war dance that good, you become a rock star. You get
groupies. The Indian women will line up to braid your hair.

No, I don't wear rubbers, he said, I want to be God and re-
populate the world in my image. I wondered, since every Indian
boy either looks like a girl or like a chicken with a big belly and
skinny legs, how he could tell which kids were his.

Anyway, he was all sexed-up from the cradle.

He used to go to Assembly of God, but when he was fifteen, he made a pass at the preacher's wife. Grabbed her tit and said, I'll save you.

Preacher man beat the shit out of him, then packed up, and left the rez forever. I felt sorry for the wife, but was happy the preacher man was gone.

I didn't like him teaching us how to speak in tongues.

Anyway, after speed came the crack and it took hold of my cousin and made him jitter and shake the dust. Earthquake—his Indian name should have been changed to Earthquake. Saddest thing: powwow regalia looks great on a too-skinny Indian man.

Then came the meth.

Indian Health Service had already taken his top row of teeth and the meth took the bottom row.

Use your drug money to buy some false teeth, I said.

I was teasing him, but he went out and bought some new choppers. Even put a gold tooth in front like some kind of gangster rapper wannabe. He led a gang full of reservation-Indians-who-listened-to-hard-core-rap-so-much-they-pretended-to-be-inner-city-black. Shit, we got fake Bloods fake-fighting fake Crips. But they aren't brave or crazy enough to shoot at one another with real guns. No, they mostly yell out car windows. Fuckers are drive-by cursing.

I heard some fake gangsters have taken to throwing government commodity food at one another.

Yeah, my cousin, deadly with a can of cling peaches.

And this might have gone on forever if he'd only dealt drugs on the rez and only to Indians. But he crossed the border and found customers in the white farm towns that circled us.

Started hooking up the Future Farmers of America.

And then he started fucking the farmers' daughters.

So they busted him for possession, intent to sell, and statutory rape. Deserved whatever punishment was coming his way.

Hey, cousin, he said to me when I visited him in jail, they're trying to frame me.

You're guilty, I said, you did all of it, and if the cops ever ask me, I'll tell them everything I know about your badness.

He was mad at first. Talked about betrayal. But then he softened and cried.

You're the only one, he said, who loves me enough to tell the truth.

But I knew he was just manipulating me. Putting the Jedi shaman mind tricks on me. I wouldn't fall for that shit.

I do love you, I said, but I don't love you enough to save you.

As the trial was cooking, some tribal members showed up at the courthouse to demonstrate. Screaming and chanting about racism. They weren't exactly wrong. Plenty of Indians have gone to jail for no good reason. But plenty more have gone to jail for the exact right reasons.

It didn't help that I knew half of those protesters were my cousin's best customers.

But I felt sorry for the protesters who believed in what they were doing. Who were good-hearted people looking to change the system. Thing is: you start fighting for every Indian, you end up having to defend the terrible ones too.

That's what being tribal can do to you. It traps you in the teepee with murderers and rapists and drug dealers. It seems everywhere you turn, some felon-in-buckskin elbows you in the rib cage.

Anyway, after a few days of trial and testimony, when things were looking way bad for my cousin, he plea-bargained his way to a ten-year prison sentence.

Maybe out in six with good behavior. Yeah, like my cousin was capable of good behavior.

Something crazy: my cousin's name is Junior Polatkin, Jr. Yes, he was named for his late father, who was Junior Polatkin, Sr. Yeah, Junior is not their nicknames; Junior is their real names. So anyway, my cousin Junior Junior was heading to Walla Walla State Penitentiary.

Junior Junior at Walla Walla.

Even he thought that was funny.

But he was terrified too.

You're right to be scared, I said, so just find all the Indians and they'll keep you safe.

But what did I know? The only thing I knew about prison was what I saw on HBO, A&E, and MSNBC documentaries.

Halfway through his first day in the big house, my cousin got into a fight with the big boss Indian.

Why'd Junior fight him?

Because he was a white man, Junior said, as fucking pale as snow.

And he had blue eyes, Junior said.

My cousin wasn't smart enough to know about recessive genes and all, but he was still speaking some truth.

Anyway, it had to be shocking to get into prison, looking for group protection, and you find out your leader is a mostly white Indian boy.

I tried to explain, my cousin said, that I was just punching the white guy in him.

Like an exorcism, I said when he called me collect from the prison pay phone. I think jail is the only place where you can find pay phones anymore.

Yeah, Junior Junior said, I was trying to get the white out of him.

But here's the saddest thing: my cousin's late mother was white. A blond and blue-eyed Caucasian beauty. Yeah, my cousin is half-white. He just won the genetic lottery when he got the black hair and brown eyes. His late brother had the light skin and pale eyes. We used to call them Sunrise and Sundown.

Anyway, my cousin lost his tribal protection pretty damn quick, and halfway through his second day in prison, he was gang-raped by black guys. And halfway through his third day, those black dudes sold Junior Junior to an Aryan dude for a carton of cigarettes.

Two hundred cigarettes for the purchase of my cousin's body and soul.

It's cruel to say, but that doesn't seem near enough. If it's going to happen to you, it should cost a lot more, right?

But what do I know about prison economics? Maybe that was a good price. Well, I guess I was hoping it was a good price. Meaning: I was mourning the shit out of my cousin's spiritual death.

Here's the thing: my cousin was pretty. He had the long black hair and the skinny legs and ass. It didn't take much to make him look womanly. Just some mascara, lipstick, and prison pants cut into ragged cutoffs.

Suddenly, I'm Miss Indian U.S.A., he said.

I'm not gay, he said.

It's not about being gay, I said, it's about crazy guys trying to hurt you as much as possible.

Jesus, he said, all these years since Columbus landed and now he's finally decided to fuck me in the ass.

Yeah, we could laugh about it. What else were we going to do? If you sing the first note of a death song while you're in prison, you'll soon be singing the whole damn song every damn day.

For the next three years, I drove down to Walla Walla to visit

Junior once or twice a month. Then it became every few months. Then I stopped driving at all. I accepted his collect calls for the first five years or so, then either he stopped calling or I stopped taking his calls. Then he disappeared from my life.

Some things just happen. Some things don't.

My cousin served his full ten-year sentence, was released on a Monday, and had to hitchhike all the way back to our reservation.

He just showed up at the tribal café as I was eating an over-cooked hamburger and greasy fries. Sat right down in the chair opposite me and smiled his bright white smile. New false teeth. Looks like he got one good thing out of prison.

Hey cousin, he said, all casual, like he'd been having dinner with me every day for the last decade.

So I said, trying to sound as casual, are you really free or did you break out?

I decided to bring my talents back to the rez, he said.

It was a hot summer day, but Junior Junior was wearing long sleeves to cover his track marks. Meaning: survival is an addiction too.

So pretty quickly we started back up our friendship. You could call us cousin-brothers or cousin–best friends. Either works. Both work. He never mentioned my absence from his prison life and I wasn't about to bring it up.

He got a job working forestry. Was pretty easy. There was nobody on the rez interested in punishing the already punished.

It's a good job, he said, I drive all the deep woods on the rez and mark trees that I think should be cut down.

Thing is, he said, we never cut down any trees, so my job is really just driving through the most beautiful place in the world while carrying a box full of spray paint.

He fell in love too, with Jeri, a white woman who worked as a nurse at the Indian Health Service Clinic. She was round and red-faced, but funny and cute and all tender in the heart, and everybody on the rez liked her. So it felt like a slice of redemption pie.

She listens to me, Junior Junior said, you know how hard that is to find?

Yeah, I said, but do you listen to her?

Junior shrugged his shoulders. Meaning: Of course I don't listen to her. I've had to keep my mouth shut for ten years. It's my turn to talk.

And talk he did.

He told me everything about how he sexed her up. Half of me wanted to hear the stories and half of me wanted to close my ears. But I didn't feel like I could stop him, either. I felt so guilty that I'd abandoned him in prison. I felt like I owed him a little bit of patience and grace.

But it was so awful sometimes. He was already sex-drunk when he went into prison, and being treated as a fuck-slave for ten years turned him into something worse. I don't have a name for it, but he talked about sex like he talked about speed and meth and crack and heroin.

She's my pusher, he said about Jeri, and her drug is her love.

Except he didn't say "love." He used another word that I can't say aloud. He reduced Jeri all the way down to the sacred parts of her anatomy. And those parts stop being sacred when you talk such blasphemy about them.

Maybe he didn't fall in love, I thought. Maybe he's time-traveling her back to prison with him.

But I also wondered what Jeri was doing with him. From the outside, she looked solid and real, like a soft dam on the river, but I guess she was a flood of shit inside. Meaning: if enough men hurt you when you're a child, you'll seek out hurtful men when you become an adult.

Talk about a Vision Quest. Jeri's spirit animal was a cannibal coyote.

Things went on like this for a couple years. He started punching her in the stomach; she hid those bruises and punched him into black eyes that he carried around like war paint.

Fucking Romeo and Juliet, my cousin said.

Yeah, like he'd ever read the book or watched any of those movies for more than ten minutes.

Then, one day, Jeri disappeared.

Rumor had it she went into one of those battered women programs. Rumor also had it she was hiding in Spokane. Which, if true, was pretty stupid. How can you hide in the City of Spokane from a Spokane Indian?

He found her in a 7-Eleven in the Indian part of town.

Yeah, as scared as she was, she was still hiding among Indians. Yeah, we're addictive. You have to be careful around us because we'll teach you how to cry epic tears and you'll never want to stop.

Anyway, you might think he wanted to kill her. Or break some bones. But no, he was crazy in a whole different way. In the aisle of that 7-Eleven, he dropped to his knees and asked for her hand in marriage.

Really.

He proclaimed it just like that too.

May I have your hand in marriage? he said to her.

So they got married; I was the best man.

In the parking lot after the ceremony, Junior and Jeri smoked meth with a bunch of toothless wonders.

Fucking zombies walking everywhere on the rez.

Monster movie all the time.

A thousand years from now, archaeologists are going to be mystified by all the toothless skulls they find buried in the ancient reservation mud.

There was no honeymoon. What rez Indian can afford such a thing? They did spend a night in the tribal casino. That's free for any Indian newlyweds. Mighty generous, I guess, letting tribal members sleep free in the casino they're supposed to own.

They moved into a trailer house down near Tshimakain Creek and they got all happy and safe for maybe six months.

Then one night, after she wouldn't have sex with him, he punched her so hard that he knocked out her front teeth.

That was it for her.

She left him and lived on the rez in plain sight. All proud for leaving, she mocked him by carrying her freedom around like her own kind of war paint. And I loved her for it.

Stand up, woman, I thought, stand up and kick the shit out of your demons.

Junior seemed to accept it okay. I should've known better, but he talked a good line of shit.

Like the poet wrote, he said, nothing gold can stay.

Robert Frost! My cousin was quoting Robert Frost! I guess he truly earned that GED he got in prison.

Late at night, when I'm trying to sleep, I think of all the ways things could have gone. How things could have been better. But in reality, there's only one way it went.

Jeri fell in love with the white dude we called Dr. Scalpel, though he went by Dr. Bob. He was the half-assed general practitioner who also worked at the Indian clinic and was just counting the days until he paid off his scholarship and could flee the rez. In the meantime, he'd found a warm body to keep him warm through the too-many-damn-Indians night.

Everybody deserves love. Well, most everybody deserves love. And Jeri certainly needed some brightness, but Dr. Bob was all dark and bitter and accelerated. He punched her in the face on their third date.

Ten minutes after we heard the news, Junior and I were speeding toward Dr. Bob's house located right next to the rez border down near the Spokane River. Yeah, he had to live on the rez, but he'd only live fifteen feet past the border.

I'm going to fuck him up, Junior said, you can't be hitting my woman.

I just rode along and never brought up the fact that Junior had hit his woman plenty of times. Yeah, I was riding shotgun for a woman-beating man looking to get revenge on another woman-beating man.

I should have been stronger. I should have been stronger. Meaning: I was kicking my face punched by my shame.

I kept thinking: Junior went to prison. He was a victim. And I ignored him. I let him suffer alone. So maybe it's okay if I let him punch Dr. Bob a few times. Maybe a little bit of violence will prevent a whole lot of violence.

But it doesn't work that way. Nowhere in human history has a small act of violence prevented larger acts from happening.

Small pain gets infected and causes big pain.

All the while he was driving, Junior was snorting whatever he could find within arm's reach. I think he snorted up some spilled sugar and salt. Any powder was good. So he was amped, he was all feedback and static, when we arrived at Dr. Bob's door.

Junior raced ahead of me and rhino-charged into the house. And once inside, he pulled a pistol from somewhere and whipped Dr. Bob across the face.

A fucking .45!

I'd seen tons of hunting rifles on the rez, but I'd never seen a pistol.

Junior whipped Dr. Bob maybe five times across the face and then kicked him in the balls and threw him against the wall. And Dr. Bob, the so-called healer, slid all injured and bloody to the floor.

You do not fuck with my possessions, Junior said to Bob.

There it was. The real reason for all of this. It was hatred and revenge, not love. Maybe at that point, all Junior could see was that Aryan who'd raped him a thousand times. Maybe Junior could only see the white lightning of colonialism. I don't mean to get so intellectual, but I'm trying to explain it to you. I'm trying to explain myself to myself.

I watched Junior lean over and slap Dr. Bob three or four times.

He's had enough, I said, let's get out of here.

Junior stood and laughed.

Yeah, he said, this fucker will never hit another woman again.

We walked toward the door together. I thought it was over. But Junior turned back, pressed that pistol against Bob's forehead, and pulled the trigger.

I will never forget how that head exploded.

It was like a comet smashing through a planet.

I couldn't move. It was the worst thing I'd ever seen. But then Junior did something worse. He flipped over the doctor's body, pulled down his pants and underwear, and shoved that pistol into Bob's ass.

Even then, I knew there was some battered train track stretching between Junior's torture in prison and this violation of Bob's body.

No more, I said, no more.

Junior stared at me with such hatred, such pain, that I thought he might kill me too. But then that moment of rage passed and Junior's eyes filled with something worse: logic.

We have to get rid of the body, he said.

I shook my head. At least I think I shook my head.

You owe me, he said.

That was it. I couldn't deny him. I helped him clean up the

blood and bone and brain, and wrap Dr. Bob in a blanket, and throw him into the trunk of the car.

I know where to dump him, Junior said.

So we drove deep into the forest, to the end of a dirt road that had started, centuries ago, as a game trail. Then we carried Bob's body through the deep woods toward a slow canyon that Junior had discovered during his tree-painting job.

Nobody will ever find the body, he said.

As we trudged along, mosquitoes and flies, attracted by the blood, swarmed us. I must have gotten bit a hundred times or more. Soon enough, Junior and I were bleeding onto Bob's body.

Blood for blood. Blood with blood.

After a few hours of dragging that body through the wilderness, we reached Junior's canyon. It was maybe ten feet across and choked with brush and small trees.

He's going to get caught up on the branches, I said.

Jesus, I thought, now I'm terrified of my own logic.

Just throw him real hard, Junior said.

So we somehow found the strength to lift Dr. Bob above our heads and we hurled him into the canyon. His body crashed through the green and came to rest, unseen, somewhere below.

Maybe you want to say a few words, Junior said.

Don't be so fucking cruel, I said, we've done something awful here.

Junior laughed again.

As we trudged back toward the car, Junior started talking childhood memories. I don't want to bore you with the details but here's the meaning: He and I, as babies, had slept in the same crib, and we'd lost our virginities on the same night within five feet of each other, and now we had killed together, so we were more than cousins, more than best friends, and more than brothers. We were the same person.

Of course, I kept reminding myself that I didn't touch Dr. Bob. I didn't pistol whip him or punch him or slap him. And I certainly didn't shoot him.

But I was still guilty. I knew that. Though I couldn't figure out exactly what I was guilty of.

When we made it back to the car, Junior stopped and stared up at the stars newly arrived in the sky.

You're going to keep quiet about this, he said.

I stared at the pistol in his hand. He saw me staring at the pistol in his hand. I knew he was deciding whether to kill me or not. And I guess his love for me, or whatever it was that he called love, won him over. He turned and threw the gun as far as he could into the dark.

We drove back down that dirt road in silence. As he dropped me at my house, he cried a little, his first sign of weakness, and hugged me.

You owe me, he said again.

After he drove away, I climbed on the roof of my house. I don't know why I did that. It seemed like the right thing to do. Folks would later call me Snoopy, and I would laugh with them, but at the time it seemed like such an utterly serious act.

I suppose, even if it became funny later, that it was the ultimate serious act.

I needed to be in a place where I had never been before to think about the grotesquely new thing that had happened, and what I needed to do about it.

I don't know when I fell asleep, but I woke, cold and wet, the next morning, climbed off the roof, and went to the tribal police. A couple hours after I told them the story, the Feds showed up. And a few hours after that, I led them all to Dr. Bob's body.

Later that night, as the police lay siege to his trailer house, Junior shot himself in the head.

No way I'm going back to prison, he said.

I wasn't charged with any crime. I could have been, I suppose, and maybe should have been. But I guess I'd done the right thing, or maybe something close enough to the right thing.

And Jeri? She left the rez, of course. I hear she's working on another rez down south. I pray that she never falls in love again. I'm not blaming her for what happened. I just think she's better off alone. Who isn't better off alone?

I didn't go to Junior's funeral. I figured somebody might shoot me if I did. Most everybody thought I was evil for turning against Junior. Meaning: I was the bad guy because I betrayed another Indian.

And yes, it's true that I betrayed Junior. But if betrayal can be righteous, then I believe I was righteous. But who knows except God?

Anyway, in honor of Junior, I started war dancing. I had to buy my regalia from a Sioux Indian who didn't give a shit about my troubles, but that was okay. I think the Sioux make the best outfits anyway.

So I danced. Well, I practiced dancing first in front of a mirror. I'd put a powwow CD in my computer and I'd stumble in circles around my living room. After a few months of this, I got enough grace and courage to make my public debut.

It was a minor powwow in the high school gym. Just another social event during a boring early December.

At first, nobody recognized me. I'd war-painted my whole face black. I wanted to look like a villain, I guess.

Anyway, as I danced, a few women recognized me and started talking to everybody around them. Soon enough, the whole powwow knew it was me swinging my feathers. A few folks jeered and threw curses my way. But most just watched me. I felt the aboriginal heat of their eyes. And I started crying. I'd like to think that I was weeping for my lost cousin, but I think I was weeping for my whole tribe.

JERRY STAHL is the author of six books, including the memoir *Permanent Midnight* (made into a movie with Ben Stiller and Owen Wilson) and the novels *I, Fatty* and *Pain Killers*. Formerly "culture" columnist for *Details*, Stahl's fiction and journalism has appeared in *Esquire*, the *New York Times*, and *The Believer*, among other places. Most recently, he wrote *Hemingway & Gellhorn*, starring Clive Owen and Nicole Kidman, for HBO. Currently, he is completing a novel, *Jumping from the H*, and working on a remake of *The Thin Man* with Johnny Depp.

# bad
## by jerry stahl

**T**HE RUSH! THE TERROR! The acrid stink of your sweat soaking through furniture three blocks away! Speaking of stink—what *is* that? Did somebody piss under your arms? Is that possible? Could they have pissed in your armpits three weeks ago, and you just now noticed? Like, say, when you get in a cab, and the seat's wet after a pack of frat boys beer-up too hard and leave Bud puddles. Hop inside and—QUESTION: *why does your God hate you?*—you hear the splat when you hit the seat. But—ANSWER: *because you're a tweaker!*—you don't know you're full wet-ass till you squish out of the cab. ("People never call the police until it's wet-ass time." Al Pacino, *Sea of Love*.) Speed keeps you so clammy you can't feel damp. Just one of the many advantages!

Fucking alcoholics! Where's the dignity? Remember that dancer—Lola? Lurleen? Patricia?—with the misspelled devil ink on her neck. *HAIL SATIN!* "It's not a mistake, it's a statement!" It *was* Lurleen. She had some kind of jailhouse harelip that slurred her words to the left. "You ass-maggot, you think I'm a fucking *creatine?*" Upscale. After eleven vodka tonics you'd see day-workers hand her five sweaty dollar bills to lift her skirt and geeze in her labia, which weirdly resembled a gorilla ear. You'd seen one once, in a French Quarter voodoo store. It was supposed to bring its owner lifelong protection and success. From the moment the Sisters of Marie Laveau Gift Shop door hissed shut behind you, you knew you should have bought the thing. Everything would have been different. Why are you such an asshole?

*Are you crying?*

Want to talk about how Lurleen (Darla? No, *Zelda)* would boot the vag-needle, let it stand up and quiver by itself, then grand finale with a Heimlich-like shudder and pass out forehead-first on the bar with the rig sticking out between her legs? The pink tip made it weirdly like a little dog's organ, aroused. (You suffer compulsive thoughts—sometimes just images—that you do not want to think, but cannot stop thinking. This is one of them.) Sometimes she'd wet herself. Who wouldn't? *"Five more bucks!"* she'd croak when she came to and saw her condition. (Remember when mysterious Chasids began to speak to you out of the ceiling? A rabbi would just appear: you'd realize you were staring at him, and that he was talking. You'd think, maybe he was *always* there. And it took THIS MUCH crystal to see him. The sad old shtetl eyes followed you from the TV as he spoke. Vaguely reassuring, vaguely menacing.) *Does your life ever feel like a continuum of one aberration, misreflected in a series of cracked rearview mirrors?* You'd think: misreflected? How lame. Then you'd rethink. He's right! Every speed-freak car you ever twitched in did have a crack in the rearview. (You once drove across the state of Utah, steering the wheel from the passenger side when the 300-pound Cherokee who picked you up hitchhiking snorted something that gave him a heart attack going ninety-five on an empty interstate. You couldn't move him, so you just steered until his husk of an Impala ran out of gas on I-15, outside of Bountiful.) All the tweak-mobiles had cracked rearview mirrors. How does that even happen *once? And how does Rabbi Bowlstein know?*

You don't even want to talk about this, but here you are, talking about it. *Keep babbling, Chatty Speed Guy. People are really into it. You're crushing them.* Sartre knew what hell was—and it wasn't other people. That's a mistranslation. His translator had the twitches from *le meth* and spilled *vin rouge* on the words *dans ta tete.* THE OTHER PEOPLE WERE IN YOUR HEAD. If you were on speed, you'd know what he knew: speed means being your own audience for the running commentary of death. Or worse than death. More of *this.* What you're feeling right now.

CRASHING 2: WHAT'S *THAT* LIKE? Remember how you felt the first time you couldn't get it up? The scalding rage. The way Cheeto-dry Cindy Carmunuci looked at you when you stopped trying to cram your sixteen-year-old shame-handle into her. Look at you. Twenty years later, the episode still has you assuming the Cringe Position. You raised your sweaty face, your eyes met hers, and she looked at you like you were some kind of a cripple. A *sex-gimp.* Crashing is that feeling. That kind of fun—some version of—nonstop. From the minute you wake up. (If you sleep, which you don't. You're not an amateur.) If you died and the coroner knew what he was doing, your cause of death would read: *Extreme Awareness.* Every conversation was toe-curling in real time, and worse when you relived it later, which you did, without surcease, even when you were having *another* conversation. There was the babbling in your head, the babbling from the person in front of you, and then all the Other Random Voices. You ceased to think. You only obsess.

WHAT PEOPLE WHO WERE NEVER ADDICTED DON'T UNDERSTAND. You did not do this shit for pleasure. You did it for relief. (Plus the voices. Did you mention them? How you'd miss them when they were not around?) *But when it*

*was working and you felt good and you were really smooook, when
every cell in the universe was humming to you, in the key of happy
hell, and you were humming with them—when that shit was going
on, and you felt abso-fucking-lutely tingly-tits optimistic . . . it was
. . . it was . . . it was . . . Shoot enough and the world whooshed to
quiet, and you were content just to sit, maybe drool a little, calm as
a hyperactive toddler after his first lick of a Ritalin lollipop. When
that happened, you never thought: "I am only this optimistic and
one-with-the-cosmos because I'm on amphetamines." When a
drug works, you don't feel like you're on a drug. You're just focused
and vaguely orgasmic. Body and brain in stunning sync, running
full-throttle. One cunthair from complete loss of control, but per-
fectperfectperfect.*

WHAT A GOOD DRUG DOES. *Is make you believe perfection
is what you are going to feel forever. Then take it away . . . Throw
you out of the cushioned fun-car onto a rocky shoulder. Shrink your
900-page thoughts back to garble. De–Dorian Gray your brain.
Which makes you go from want to need. ("Maybe things weren't
moving fast, or maybe things were moving too fast. I don't even
remember anymore. I had it made. And I woke up. One morning. I looked down. And fell off my life." Paul Newman, WUSA.
Screenplay by Robert Stone.) This is what's making crashing so
. . . uncomfortable. So disappointing. So—ARE YOU STILL
TALKING?* Remember the fake punk in Berlin who bit off his
finger?

Be honest, Sparkle-pony, how's your life going? Really? Have
you looked in the mirror lately? No, really looked. Good for you.
Hold onto that magic.

(Of course you have ADHD. It's not like there's not a medical

reason to stand in a puddle and stick your finger in a socket.)
You were talking about—what was her name? Not Lurleen,
now that you think of it, it was something showbiz . . . Dee-Lay!
Dee-Lilah! Dee-Neero, maybe? One of Dee-Neero's through-
the-pantie shots ended up abscessing—giving her what she
called "cauliflower vagina." "That's pretty good," you said. And
she said she had a degree in English, but they didn't pay her to
talk about Chaucer with her thong pulled sideways. Which—it
made sense at the time—led to her splashing the customers way
before the "Squirt Craze." Which you found out about thanks to
the social elixir that was quality trailer-park methamphetamine.
Which—are you going to do this all fucking night? Speed never
made you smarter. It just let you be what you already were longer. It turbocharged stupid. (The weird thing about Dee, you
just remembered, was that she wanted to have a stroke. *"Like,
if I can shut off my whole left brain, it'd be just fucking BLISS."*)
Her sometime boyfriend Donnie, who might have also been her
brother, but said he was her agent, spent five hours explaining
how he actually thought up the "Squirt" concept in your dealer's
doublewide; a model so spectacularly lush it had a hot tub. Donnie was one of those Valley porn guys who had gone into "lawn
care." Strictly legit. But still. Drunk, with some crank flecks in
his *Magnum, P.I.* crumb-catcher, he'd go all misty-eyed. Sigh
right at you over the tub-scum frothing his chin. You weren't
supposed to get into hot tubs on amphetamines. Guys got heart
attacks. So Donnie told you. A little too enthusiastically. "Time
it well, you go right to the edge, kiss a coronary on the mouth
. . ." Then, wrapped in a beach towel, he'd pull out his wallet
and unfold a yellowed issue of the long defunct *L.A. Reader*. (He
did this more than once, pretty much nightly.) Once he unfolded
and smoothed it, he'd let you see the picture of him, the cover
story, young and smiling, wearing the same hair as Harry Reems,

posed in a Hawaiian shirt with his arm around what may or not may not have been an underage Tahitian woman. In the photo her red nails were visible, fingers wrapped up to the mouth blow-job-style around a swirly-glassed green bottle of old-fashioned Squirt soda pop. The headline's in BOLD LETTERS over his Reems hair: *NOT YOUR FATHER'S SQUIRT.* Under the soft drink, in smaller print, the kicker*: Is it marketing if my new wife does it?* Below that—and you remember, because you knew the guy whose uncle laid out the cover, a total crankaholic whose aorta was going to pop on a bus in three years—below that, in the so-small-only-speedfreaks-would-notice thought balloon super-imposed over the Belle of the South Pacific: *Would you believe it, my little Roxy can write her name on the ceiling!* (There is a world of secret messages when you're really hitting the pep pills. Reality is a crossword puzzle you can solve in your head—until you forget what words are.)

It's like you're outside and it's ten in the morning, and the sun is just scorching the rubber T-shirt you never saw before in your life. Which you realize after you've been peeling it off for half a day is actually your skin. You take a deep breath, groan out a rush that makes your fingernails itch, and suddenly dialogue that explains everything is projected in the sky. The letters remind you of your father's eyes, except you don't feel the seething. *This is what this means,* the letters say. *That is what that means.* Did you mention how sometimes your eyes bleed? You could write a book about bleeding eyeballs. *The more that wants more wants more, and the more that can't do anymore wants more too.* One day you wake up and you're letting your appetite sign your checks. You know that feeling? What was my name again?

# IN THE DE-SPEED WING

DAY ONE. You write a poem with doorbell and cerebellum appearing in the same sentence thirty-six times. They give you something for the shakes and put an ice cube in your mouth, which cracks badly at the corners. Your blood appears to be plaid.

DAY TWO. A counselor later to become famous in a rehab reality show keeps asking you in group what "your deal" is. After the fifth time, when he's standing right over you, you finally start to answer and he laughs and yells in your face from two inches away. *"Bullshit!"* It's not your fault there are secret webs between things; that with enough amphetamine in your system, you see DEEP AND MEANINGFUL PATTERNS among seemingly random phenomena. How it all CONNECTS. After that you think—*So what?*

You are tired of not being a centipede. You just want a patch of dirt, somewhere you do not have to keep pretending to know how to be human.

DAY THREE. Circle the date, you're well enough for restraints! A Kush-breath orderly straps you chest-and-ankles over the gurney blanket, then wheels you down the hall. He leans in, like he wants to smell you, so close you know if you inhale you're going to test positive for something. Maybe THC, maybe chlamydia. He kind of smile-whispers: *"The first word in boundaries is bound!"* His voice is half hard-core speedfreak, half twink Widmark, psycho-giggly Tommy Udo pushing an old wheelchair lady down the stairs. (Most people only have one half. Once you realize that, life is not necessarily easier, but it's explainable.) *They put fluorescent lights in the elevator to make you epileptic, then cure you with expensive stimulants.*

DAY FOUR. You see the albino. He had some kind of paint-thinner-methedrine incident in his mother's carnival. Grabbing men and women's palms on the midway, reading them and weeping: *You don't fucking want to know!* You can't remember if he's the one who hung himself or became regional vice president of Nabisco South America.

*Once you start trying to control your feelings, you have already lost control.* Shame is like a rush in the wrong direction. Are you saying you've never wanted to obliterate the history of your own mind? There was a rumor: the guy who really burned down the L.A. downtown library on April 29, 1986 was a peckerhead tweaker trying to fry Jews and Mexicans out of his brainpan. But that was then.

This is now: You climb Everest, then you do laundry for the rest of your life. (The first time you go to a laundromat, without speed, you hate that the spinning laundry is boring . . . It used to explain the universe. That's how you knew you were really off speed. You had no fucking clue about the universe, except that it made you self-conscious. Speed and laundromats. Because sometimes you just have to do something. And washing clothes is always the right thing to . . .)

*Describe "the burden of nonstop awareness." Why? Just go look at the lights at Rite-Aid at four in the morning, when it's just you and the eighty-year-old security man watching a hunched-up guy with shades and a leg brace screw the top off his Robitussin DM, guzzle half a bottle like it's Thunderbird, then smack his lips and take off his sunglasses. Eyes that peeled back don't come without a lot of speed-work. You recognize each other like Masons. The pharmacist, whose nametag says* Bairj Donabedian, *stares at you and picks up a telephone. When did life get this good?*

*ALL FUCKED OUT AND STILL AWAKE.* Why is everything you remember bad? Now it comes back to you. What was her name? The ex-lawyer who dragged her little boy to the motel. Gave the kid an already-colored-in Yogi Bear coloring book? Even after the boy'd gone through half the book, he still had this hopeful look on his face before he turned every page. You were all in this motel room with a dozen other versions of you. All white guys. All waiting. But you couldn't help notice this kid. Every time he turned a page on that coloring book, he had his crayon in the air, ready to go. And every time, he was just *shattered* when he saw that it was already colored on. *Have you ever seen a five-year-old age?*

You were just there to cop. But you saw anyway. Each filled-in Yogi and Boo-Boo killed the kid a little more . . . Watching this, even your cells hated themselves . . . (Just because you give somebody something for the first time doesn't make you responsible if what you give them destroys their entire life. Does it?) Carmine—that was her name. *Why do you do this to yourself?* Carmine gave the child to the grinning simp in the cowboy hat. And what did you do? (You could have said something. You didn't. If you were staring straight at a pedophile—and there had to be at least a *chance*—if you *were*, you had other priorities. But still . . .) There's right behavior. And behavior that's right on methamphetamine. You did your job! You took advantage—of *empathy!* You glared at the little boy's mother—if Carmine really was his mother, and not his pimp! You registered the youngster's wince when Smiling Cowboy Man plopped a hand on his hunched-up, scared-shitless little-boy shoulders. But while you glowered at the woman who handed him to strangers, as if she were somehow morally reprehensible, what did you do? You stole. You wet-fingered a wedge of fresh meth off the motel desk like you practiced with a speed-thief trainer. You glowered at Carmine while you stole her drugs. It was a kind of morality. Was it stealing if they didn't know you did it? How much of your mental activity is spent worrying what other people can see? Is it pathology? Or is it Memorex?

OBLIVION HAS NO NARRATIVE. Just because there's no plot does not mean the story can't get worse.

After questionable man and boy left, Carmine (Britt), who must have been triple-jointed, brazenly lifted a bare dirt-crusted foot up to her nose *unassisted*. She sniffed a filthy toe—as if, you thought, to see if you were a dirty-toe man—then hissed at you. *"Don't give me that look. Dewey happens to be Dewey Junior's daddy! And don't think I don't know what you are, neither. God made a lower place in hell for lowlife drug thieves than kiddie diddlers."*

Is it normal to keep remembering horrible things? It's not your fault they keep happening. Remember? That tweaked-out voice low as the hell pit he was describing. "It's in the Bible." Did you dream the evangelist? Or is he in the walls? This is a question you didn't used to ask yourself. *"Ladies and gentlemen, I want you all to look in your heart, ask yourself this question. Is your life nothing more than a history of saying yes to the wrong things?"* Can zombies be sad?

THE ESKIMO WITH HOOKS FOR HANDS LOOKED

UNFAMILIAR, BUT HE SAID HE WAS A VET. He was shooting up Penny, who you couldn't remember meeting, in the neck. While you watched, her jugular wriggled like a worm in cookie dough, cracking the makeup she used to cover up vein-puff. "It's important," she said, while the shooter dabbed her off, "I'm a nurse. People can see our necks." The story doesn't track. But speed stories never track. They only make sense if you're on speed. (This is a test.) At what point did the Inuit show up with the vial of liquid meth? "What you staring at?" The big-faced musher was eyeballing you, clicking his hooks. You screamed, *"Get the fuck out of here!"* and he backed away. Was he laughing? Maybe he didn't leave. Impossible to tell what was going on; everything three-day-up echoey. Maybe the Eskimo just went in the bathroom. Maybe they were married. Maybe she brought him white assholes to kill after she fucked them in front of him. Maybe she killed them after *he* fucked them. Shit. Why does all your energy go into panic? Except for everything you knew about her, Penny seemed almost normal. Like a cheerleader who slept outside.

NOT EVERYBODY KNOWS YOU CAN BLACK OUT ON SPEED. You can be unconscious and chatty at the same time. Flip back from a clammy sense-memory of Mommy-flesh to an IHOP booth beside a plus-size ironic shemale busy not eating her Belgian waffles. Miss Waffle is still talking when you rematerialize, when your star falls from the night sky over Methlehem. To reenter the earth's BO. Boring Orbit. *"What was that movie? They Shoot Horses, Don't They? Well, screw the ponies! I shoot the same go-fast that made Hitler, Sartre, Lucille Ball, and Philip K. Dick complete geniuses!"* Plus-size Tranny-pants cannot stop talking. Mouth moving in a face dead as the papier-mâché Belgian waffles in the IHOP display case. *"Listen up, 'kay? I don't mind payin' for the party, but you gotta at least look interested! My husband had a thing where he'd drop Black Beauties and touch himself. He wouldn't eat dinner. That was the tell. I'd peep him cracking open ten black capsules on rice puddin' and gulpin' it down. Then he'd put his hands on me, rough, all over, like he want-ed to pull out my organs and dunk them in coffee. Ooooooooooooh! It was goddamn heaven."* You stay fake-interested. Long enough to burn through what's left of a crappy eight ball wedged between the honey bear and the teapot. Nobody at IHOP gives a shit. It's IHOP. It's five after fucked-up o'clock in the morning. Just as you get up, Miss Waffles blurts, *"You can't hide, I can read your mind in nine languages."*

You are eye level with a case of textbook meth-lips. So dry each syllable launches a tiny bursting pillow of speed feathers, which drift down to the Bondo-like untouched whipped cream below. *"Know why sexual relations on speed are so twisted?"* She makes a here-comes-the-funny face. *"Sexual relations! Listen to me! I stay up for a day and a half and suddenly I'm NPR!"* She lets out a pained giggle. (It's a meth tic—the pain giggle. All emotions are a shade of suffering, once you're beyond the ecstatic.)

When there's nothing else, you can love people just from know-ing they suffer too. It hits right and you feel that vast, inchoate empathy. *How would you describe yourself at such "peak" mo-ments. "Crippled and happy about it."* But there you go, bragging!

*It's different when you do it with somebody else.* Like when your hefty transgender friend says, "I think I hear a lump in my breast. Is that possible?" You nod with Real Concern, edging slowly backward away from the booth. Stimulants stimulate everybody: even the people near you. Beehived IHOP waiters just know, and they stay out of the way. (It's IHOP.) When she yells, you feel the eyes of family diners. "Thief!" Waffles warbles. "Thief. There he goes! *Thief!*" You keep your head down. The screams follow you. "You think if you keep moving backward, you can make your life unhappen? Smell yourself!"

(The shit helps you feel nothing. But not nothing enough.)

IN THE OLD DAYS, YOU HAD A SPONGE TEST. When the floor got spongy, you knew. You'd gone too far. Time to come back! Swallow a Valium. Swallow nine. Drink some mouthwash. You need *something*. By the time you hit Sponge Mode, reality feels fraught and menacing. (Could be two days up, could be twelve.) Regardless. Your life is reduced to walking the yard in a maximum-security bouncy house. Your heart hurts. You catch yourself talking out loud, explaining deranged sensations to strangers in the street. "My motel room hates me."

*CAJANK!* There is a girl in your room who won't stop scream-ing. Candy? Kembra? Cathy? Caroline? . . . *Crickle?* When you walk in she stops screaming and gets solicitous. Which is scarier than screaming. She could be twenty-three or forty. "Are you shivering, mister, or is that a convulsion?"

*Kimberly!* That was her name. The one with the diapers. You didn't dream this. You were geezing this evil-smelling grit you bought from a plumber in Bakersfield. Bathtub crank with a Drano after-drip. Kimberly says she bought special diapers with holes in them. Fuck-me diapers. Remember? Oooh, I wore my Sex Depends. Just for you!

This, you realized later, was *another* lie. Kimberly! Speedfreaks always lie. The diapers weren't REALLY called Sex Depends. She slit the crotch with a razor. Then she used felt-tip pens, magic markers to color faces on the diapers. Fifty-three tiny faces. (Look, there's Ringo! There's Abraham Lincoln. There's Helen Keller! There's you!) It took her days. Gink-work. That's how she made them. She had lots of razors 'cause she was also a cutter. Of course. Little Girl Cutters grow up to be Big Girl Speedfreaks.

Right, right, right, right, right, right, right. Doctors gave her Adderall for the cutting. Why wouldn't they? Adderall helped her focus on the H she was slicing in her forehead. H? *Stands for HELL, douche-lame!* And, right in front of you, she starts cutting her thighs. Sees you looking. Then explains. Amped-up and serene. "Cutting's better than picking. Last Christmas I picked a hole in my cheek you could put your finger through!"

God, she is screaming right in your face. Can bad breath give you cancer?

"In New Orleans," she tells you huskily, "you put the crystal in your eye. They call it Les Yeux-Yeux. Cajuns call it Cajank." She also said her mother used to eat her father's ball-hair. Every morning, after he shaved, Papa would snip at his scrotum beard. And when he was done, her mother would make her come into the bathroom and help her gather up the tiny hairs. She'd put them in a glass of water, swirl it a little, then drink up. Clarence Thomas style. "Mama say no woman will want Daddy when she's got his pubes in her belly. Mama knew things." Now it sounds weird. But then—with the light on the white walls shimmering the blood sloshing off the top of your skull, it made tremendous sense. It made you sob. (You had to keep reminding yourself to breathe; every moment felt either really right or really wrong.)

Miss New Orleans told you the only reason she did speed was that her mother made her take "zese leetle capsools" so she could see better when they searched for Daddy-hair. Mama gave the little girl Dexedrine, just like little Judy Garland got. She'd spend the day studying every square inch of bathroom floor instead of going to school. When she found a curl she'd yelp and Mommy would give her a smooch. She covered her eyes as she told the story. She hugged her knees. Then the tears would come and she'd need something. What are mommies for?

*STOP THINKING ABOUT DISEASE.* That's how you get one. It's so fucking hard to breathe. Speedfreaks get sick. Not you. You're not one of them. You're different. You're never going to get a disease. Even though you've been up for . . . a while. You're not one of them. You're different. You still brush your teeth. (Manually now, since you took your Waterpik apart.) You floss. You even urinated. Maybe two days ago.

Your heartbeat could set off car alarms. How many days? What do insects feel when they fuck? Max Jacobson gave injections to Truman Capote, Tennessee Williams, Eddie Fisher, Mother Teresa, and JFK, who was so reliant on Dr. Max—a.k.a. Feelgood— he flew him to summits, like the B1 in Austria. With Khrushchev. Jack wanted to stay sharp.

Dr. J had amphetamine getaways for VIPs in his splash-pad on East 53rd. He made tapes. Wouldn't you? After three days, everybody's a pervaloid. There's Tennessee, wearing Mother Teresa's surprisingly plush, high-rise undergarments. "If I wore these, they'd call *me* mother!"

YOUR GRANDFATHER HAD A SCANDAL INVOLV-

ING INHALERS. He got caught soaking Benzedrine cotton inhalers in coffee and drinking it with the other degenerates in Times Square. Before he moved back to Cleveland, missing his teeth, Gramps had his pocket picked by Herbert Huncke, also high on Bennies. Each time you share this, which you forget that you made up, you bust your buttons. But all your stories are from long ago. Even the true ones.

You are normal. It's the speed that made you a freak.

# PART II
## machination

*Tex LeBeauf*

SCOTT PHILLIPS is the author of six
novels, including *The Ice Harvest*
and, most recently, *The Adjustment*
(Counterpoint) and *Nocturne* (les
Éditions la Branche). He lives in St.
Louis, MO.

# labiodental fricative
## by scott phillips

### torie

So you want to know something weird about Jerry?" I ask. Glen stops licking for a second and I immediately regret it. "Huh?"

"Get your face back down there, big boy." He starts up again, not the best head I've ever had but better than Jerry anyway. Better than none. "He has a tooth fetish."

He stops licking again and starts laughing.

"Get back to it," I tell him, "I'm just about ready." We're in the backseat of Glen's Lexus, which is pretty fucking sweet, even if he is living in it. When he first told me he was driving one I thought he was full of shit, because he looked like a guy who lived in a dumpster or maybe just a grove of trees down by the river. Or beneath an underpass or in a refrigerator box.

And while I can hardly believe I'm letting him go down on me like this, I also can't believe he's doing it so enthusiastically, because to be perfectly honest, I left Jerry's in kind of a rush this morning and I don't know exactly what it's like down there, but I'm experiencing that not-so-fresh feeling, if you know what I mean. I get the feeling he just wants to fuck me so bad he's willing to go through a lot for it, which is kind of romantic when you think of it, and he knows perfectly well why I'm doing it: because I know he's holding and right now Jerry isn't and inside Glen was hinting that he had a lead on a whole bunch of it and that was why he was trying to sell Jerry that penis back at the bar.

I'm getting tired of listening to the little animal noises he's making, like he thinks there's something sexy about being gone down on by a big old slobbery bear, and anyway I'm never going to come so I make some reasonably convincing orgasm noises and pull him up and in, and thank Christ it only takes him about fifteen seconds to come, which is when it occurs to me that I should have made him wear a condom and probably a dental dam too, because Christ only knows what a guy like him has swimming around on his tongue.

So anyway, he's pulling his pants back up, at which point I become aware of a pretty gamy odor that I realize is coming from his crotch, and I have to hold my breath until he gets buckled back up again, and even then it lingers like foreign cheese in the back of the Lexus, which has real leather seats, probably standard equipment, and he says, "What was that about a fetish?"

"Tooth fetish. I'm a dental hygienist."

"I thought you managed Furry's."

"I do. I *used to be* a hygienist, is what I should have said, and the first time Jerry met me he said what a beautiful big mouth I had, and I almost hit him because I'm sensitive about the size of my teeth, but I could see he was totally serious so I took it as sweet instead of, you know, insulting. So how'd you get hold of Dean Martin's penis anyway?"

## jerry

The first time I saw Torie I was a lost cause. Big, round eyes, incisors prominent enough that her lips are slightly parted when her face is at rest, like she's just about to say something. Thick, wavy black hair, a long, aquiline nose, and perfect olive skin. I knew right then I'd follow her anywhere. Which is how Torie ended up managing the bar instead of cleaning other people's less attractive teeth, and living in my condo instead of at home with her husband and three kids. As well as snorting me out of house and home, which is a hard thing for me to complain about since I was the one got her started on crank when we first started partying together.

She used to come in with her friends and fellow hygienists after work. A couple of times when she stayed late, long after the other girls went home, we had deep discussions about life—hers, mostly—and its attendant disappointments—again, mainly hers. One night her husband came by to get her, and he made it clear that he didn't consider this the kind of place where a decent Christian wife and mother ought to be spending her evenings.

But the band was playing, and she'd been dancing and having a good time, and she had no intention of leaving. We had the Jake Hornor Blues Band playing every second Friday and Saturday of the month back then, best draw I ever had, and this was the third time I'd let her sample a little bit of what Larry the dishwasher had been selling me (and a good portion of my staff and clientele) for the last couple years. When hubby grabbed her upper arm on the dance floor to drag her out to her car, she swung at him with the other fist and the whole thing ended up with Kurt—that's the husband—eighty-sixed and thinking he was lucky I didn't bring the cops in on his ass. (I make it a rule never to call the cops unless we've been robbed, but he didn't know that.)

She lost her hygienist job a couple of months after, over chronic lateness and absenteeism. I hired her on as a waitress, and when she turned out not to have that in her, I just made her a manager and let her earn a living being hot.

And then a year and a half had gone by, and I'd gotten into the business of distribution myself, with Larry the dishwasher promoted to ID checker/procurer, and Torie had gotten herself seriously skinny. She was never a big girl, but by the time my old buddy Glen came in after two or three years' absence, she was getting, to these old eyes, a wee bit cadaverous.

Apart from his eyes being so bulbous, red, and wet, Glen might himself have passed for a corpse of a couple weeks' standing as he leaned on the bar and lectured me about how badly the place had gone downhill since the last time he was in. "Who you got playing this weekend?" he asked. "Heard Hornor won't play here anymore; says you stiffed him."

"He's a fucking liar. I won't book him anymore—he showed up drunk three times in a row and I fired his ass." This was true, though he played just fine when he was drunk. I had stiffed him twice, though I still had every intention of paying him what I owed. "Got the Jimmie Kralik Trio coming in."

"Fuck that, those guys couldn't draw a crowd to a public hanging," Glen said. He couldn't quit looking at Torie, who in turn was pretending he wasn't there.

Watching someone else ogle your girl ought to make you see her afresh, it seems to me, maybe renew your ardor, but whatever Glen was seeing wasn't there for me anymore. All I saw right then was how sunken her cheeks were looking, how stringy and lank her hair had gotten (she was way past due for a perm), how she didn't braid it up anymore. That beautiful olive complexion was veering toward the greenish and she was breaking out with zits that I had to keep pointing out because she didn't notice them herself. I'd been thinking about scaring up a little weed in hopes of getting her appetite up, maybe just enough to keep the weight she had on if not gain some of it back. Right about then I wouldn't have minded that husband of hers showing up and taking her back to the house and kids, which he'd quit trying to do about six months after she bailed on the whole failing enterprise.

"Got a business proposition for you," Glen said. He was a lawyer, or had been at any rate, and he'd presented me with opportunities in the past that hadn't turned out too badly, as well as a few others I knew enough to steer clear of. This was the first time I'd seen him since he'd headed up to Portland, Oregon, to help his brother run a rehabilitation facility for the blind and speechless or some such charity scam.

Torie snorted and turned away. I could understand, seeing Glen the way he looked now and never having experienced Glen the prosperous attorney: glad-hander Glen, buyer of rounds, purveyor of free legal advice to the indigent, ladies' man, bon vivant. This Glen looked like he could use a hot meal and a good night's sleep somewhere besides the backseat of his car. I poured him a shot and slid it in front of him; since he hadn't asked for one I assumed he didn't have the money to pay for it.

"On me," I said. "Welcome home."

"Much appreciated." He slammed it and set the glass back down on the table, then extracted from his inside jacket pocket a cardboard box. "Behold," he said, opening it to reveal what looked like a piece of beef jerky resting on a bed of cotton.

"Nice," I said.

"You know what I have here?"

"Looks like a dried-up turd," Torie said, her voice now raspy as any grizzled barfly's.

"Ladies and gentlemen," Glen announced in what I imagine was a weak echo of his erstwhile courtroom vocal style, "for your amusement and edification, the johnson of the Chairman of the Board."

"His what, now?"

"This is the mummified penis of Mr. Francis Albert Sinatra."

## torie

I'm starting to get nervous because I'm all of a sudden conscious of the parking lot lights shining into the back of the Lexus.

"Jesus, who'd want to buy Dean Martin's cock?"

"Frank Sinatra's, get it straight."

"Whatever," I shrug, thinking it's no wonder Glen's not married, he hasn't said anything sweet to me since he came, the kind of things a lady likes to hear after intercourse, like *You have really pretty lashes* or *Your hair smells terrific* or *God, your boobs look good in the moonlight*, things like that. Anyway, I press the matter, thinking it has something to do with the meth. "Okay, Sinatra's junk, then, where'd you get it?"

"Guy sold it to me in the bar of a Mexican restaurant in Palm Desert. Said they'd had to disinter him for some kind of maintenance—the concrete seal was broken on the vault or some such thing—and while he was above ground they were storing the remains inside the mortuary. So this guy broke Frank's dick off and kept it for a couple years as a lucky charm."

"Huh."

"And as a lucky charm it didn't do him much good, because when I met him he was really hurting for some crank and I happened to be holding, so I traded him, and afterward it occurs to me that this might be worth some change. And when I hit town today, just by coincidence, I run into my old friend Chuck who wants to know do I know anybody who's got five hundred dollars, 'cause he's got himself several cases of store-brand cold medicine that just fell off a loading dock."

I don't believe there's any such thing as a coincidence and I tell him that I think Frank Sinatra's leaky vault and Chuck's case of cold medicine and Glen's and my meeting and Jerry being out of crank all coming together at once are a plan of the cosmos, which is the kind of thing I never would have said a few years ago but which I truly believe now, having experienced too many weird juxtapositions of reality over the last couple of years to take any of these signs and wonders for granted.

"Does that mean you've got five hundred?" he asks.

The truth is, I have about seventy-five bucks in my checking, because I have to pay child support, if you can believe that, to my ex-husband Kurt, who has an $80,000-a-year job in franchise relations at Pizza Hut, while I'm making $23,000 and change working for my cheapskate boyfriend, which Kurt knows perfectly well and so does his lawyer and so does the judge, but they're all about making me pay for being a runaway mom. Believe me, if the situation was reversed there'd be divorced dads support groups all over the case, but believe me too when I say nobody likes a runaway mom, especially when the youngest one wasn't even talking yet when I left and Kurt has trained her to call me Torie instead of Mommy, and Kurt's new wife Perfect Stacia gets called Mommy. Stacia who totally had her sights set on Kurt way, way before I split, who was licking her chops like a Doberman eyeing a three-legged kitten when she heard I'd blown. Like I give a shit anyway.

"We could get it," I tell him.

## glen

My first thought was: kill Jerry and make it look like a stickup, take the money and the woman both. Jerry's always treated me like a schmuck, even when I've helped him out of a couple of legal scrapes, including one serious count of selling liquor to a minor. That one was no walk in the park, and all he did when it was over was piss and moan about the bribe money he'd had to lay out. And then there was the question of Frank Sinatra's desiccated organ. I was tweaking when I got hold of it, and I'd been tweaking ever since, and Jerry's dismissive attitude slammed home the obvious fact that I had no way to prove whose junk I was carrying, short of calling up Frank Jr. and asking for a DNA sample. The fantasy mountain of pure crystal and pussy and cash created by the tectonic activity of my overstimulated cerebral cortex collapsed instantaneously into a crevasse of despair and cheap-ass street meth. I had hit the wall, and just as I was running out of crank.

Yeah, I could have killed Jerry with no compunctions.

## chuck

It is easy enough, I suppose, to underestimate the intelligence of a man who sells pot next to a dumpster behind the Choose'n'Save, especially for someone like Glen, who thinks himself a sharpy in the vein of a Hugh Hefner or a Warren Beatty or a Gary Hart. You know the kind I mean. When he sees a woman that pleases his eye he sets that eye on her until his filthy ends are met, then he loses interest in that particular lady who no doubt is or was the most precious flower of another. He did this to my own precious flower six years ago, when my girlfriend Gretchen was facing a charge of possession with intent to distribute.

Marijuana. *Cannabis sativa*. I was a slave to it as much as to her at that time; the fact that she had an ounce and a half of it on her person upon her arrest was strictly due to my own baleful influence. Enter, in the outward guise of savior, my friend (I thought) Glen, hotshot attorney and drinking buddy, occasional purchaser of my wares. He worked the case without recompense, for which I was grateful.

Then, six months later, Gretchen and I were going at it hammer and tongs over her little dachshund Tami's tendency to shit in my loafers—I did hate that awful farting bitch something fierce—when she pulled out the big rhetorical guns and announced that yes, in fact, Glen had charged a fee, and that it had involved her mouth and his organs of regeneration. I threw her and Tami out. Ever since I have been waiting for the moment (never really believing it would come) when I might pay Glen back for his perfidy.

## torie

Jerry keeps a couple of grand in cash taped to the underside of his sock drawer, which is stupid. Right? Isn't that stupid? That's the kind of guy Jerry is. Smart and stupid both, sometimes in the same sentence.

## glen

The woman was a mess and she smelled like chicken soup and swamp water, but she was the first human female in close to a year who'd consented to lay with me free of charge and I wasn't about to fuck that up, especially when she looked ready to fly the coop on Jerry. It cost me the last of my meager stash to get her out to the Lexus, where I explained to her about the five hundred dollars and the cold medicine. She didn't have it, she told me, and she pointed out that if we borrowed the money from Jerry unawares we wouldn't owe anything, either in terms of cash or product.

"I like the way you think," I told her, although what I saw in her was less thought than a kind of low animal cunning, a hillbilly slyness that made the betrayal of her boss and lover as natural and uncomplicated as switching brands of toothpaste.

We were driving out on Hydraulic headed for a supermarket. It was closed at that hour but the security guard let Chuck do some business out behind the dumpsters in return for modest monetary and pharmaceutical compensation. I'd known Chuck for twenty years, and despite a reckless and fearless way of doing business, he'd never been in any major trouble. A lack of guile and considerable personal charm had gotten him out of many a scrape, and a lack of ambition had kept him out of the bigger leagues where he probably would have gotten himself killed.

The female was talking about teeth, a subject she probably should have avoided. First of all, hers were huge and starting to get meth gray, despite her claims that she still brushed and flossed thrice daily. Second, nobody wants to hear about that kind of shit from a dental hygienist even when they're a captive audience in the chair, let alone when they've got an ongoing criminal enterprise they're trying to concentrate on.

"You ever hear of meth mouth?" I asked her, hoping she'd get the picture and shut the fuck up. No such luck. She went into lecture mode, expounding at length about her personal theory that meth mouth was a result of tweakers neglecting their flossing because they were too distracted by the getting and consuming of their drug of choice and not because of the drug's unorthodox chemical manufacturing process itself.

"Look at me," she said. "I've been doing this for like a year or more and my teeth are as beautiful and straight as they've ever been."

I agreed, but just because I thought I might want more access to her person later.

"So where are we going to sell this cold medicine once we get it?" she asked.

I had an idea, I told her, a friend of a friend up in Topeka went by the name of Crumdog, sergeant-at-arms for a bikers' organization.

"So how come this Chuck guy wants to sell it to you?" she asked. "Wouldn't he make better money selling it to some cook? Doesn't he know anybody?"

"You sure do ask a lot of questions," I said, trying not to sound like I was thinking about backhanding her.

## jerry

God, I hated seeing what had become of Glen. I ignored the maybe-penis in the box and glanced back at Torie, who was still looking down her nose at him.

"So what happened to the home for the blind and deaf?"

"Well, my brother had some licensing issues with the state of Oregon, we never quite got it open, and then my girlfriend kicked me out. Blah blah blah, long story short, I'm back here. But I still got the Lexus."

"That's good."

"So how much for Frank's pecker?"

"Nothing, Glen."

"Nothing? For a relic that's seen the insides of Ava Gardner and Mia Farrow both?"

Just then Matt Sweeney walked in. He used to be a doctor, so I waved him over for a quick look. "That a human penis, Matt?"

He stuck out his lower lip and took the box from Glen. "Hard to say. Could be. You'd have to show a pathologist."

"How much, man?" Glen was whining now.

"Nothing. Even if that is a human penis, it's not Sinatra's."

"Prove it!" Glen shouted.

"Calm down now, pal," I said. "What makes you think it's worth anything, anyway, even if it is Ol' Blue Eyes' John Thomas?"

I could see his fantasy beginning to implode inside his skull. "You could charge money to see it. They auctioned Napoleon's off for big bucks."

"There's no proof. You'd have to show provenance. A chain of custody. Where'd you get it, anyway?"

## chuck

When I ran into him at the Brass Candle, trying to get someone to buy him a drink without actually lowering himself to asking for one, Glen looked like a cat had done its business in his mouth. There was a slight pleasure in the recognition that I was now doing better than he, so I bought him a beer and a shot and he asked me how was Gretchen. It was the half-hidden leer I perceived that made my pity, such as it was, evaporate.

"Last I heard she was in jail for soliciting."

Did I enjoy the look of shock on his sagging face? I did for a moment, until I realized that there was no guilt in it, that he bore no sense of his own responsibility in this tragic matter. Though I am long out of the narcotics trade, it was plain Glen wasn't, and seeing my long-awaited shot at comeuppance, I asked him if he knew anyone who wanted in on a score.

His eyes narrowed as if he was already trying to figure out how to screw me out of the score I was generously letting him in on. "Might be I'd be interested," he said.

"For five hundred I can get five cases of store-brand pseudo-ephedrine," I said.

"I got something right here on my person worth a fuckload more than five hundred, and I'd trade you outright." He reached into the inside pocket of his coat, and I put my hand on his arm, shaking my head no.

"Cash only," I told him, which got him real quiet.

"You going to be out behind the Choose'n'Save dumpster tonight?" he asked.

"Fuck yeah, every night," I said, reverting to an exaggerated version of my former manner of speaking. In catching up with him I had deliberately skipped the uplifting "can-do" parts of my redemption story: the associate's degree in English, the pretty happy marriage to Bonnie—who is a nurse's aide and disapproves of any and all illicit drug use—and especially the assistant manager job at the very same Choose'n'Save behind which I once dealt dope.

## torie

As soon as we got the money we went over to Larry the dishwasher's house and scored, then we headed out toward the supermarket where Glen's friend would be waiting with the cold meds. In the heady rush of new love Glen and I both maybe overdid the snorting, but God, it felt good. I'd packed my bag with all the clothes and jewelry I thought I'd need in my future life as Mrs. Glen Frobe.

Did I feel bad about taking Jerry's $2,565? Nope. The gun in his night table? A little, because what if someone broke in and there was Jerry scrambling for the weapon in the drawer and it's not there and he gets killed and his last thoughts are, *That conniving thieving bitch took my fucking piece and I loved her more than anything I ever loved, goddamnit,* while the intruders, bikers as I'm imagining them, cut off his slim-as-a-pea-shoot pecker and do all manner of horrid things to him in an orgy of speed-fueled sadism that lasts until one of the bikers, I'm imagining his name is Seth or something else biblical—I know: Esau!—says something like, "Shit, man, this is one dead motherfucker," and they go rooting around looking for whatever they can scavenge since Jerry never has much dope lying around the house and the money taped under the drawer is gone, another thing Jerry probably would be cursing me for, even as he reflects that he's never loved anybody like he loved me, with my prominent overbite and my twenty minutes of Kegels every day.

## jerry

Soon as I saw something going on between Torie and Glen I sensed a golden opportunity, because Glen is a guy who can't say no to a piece of ass and Torie will do anything to get high, and when she made an excuse to leave five minutes after he headed out the door I had that magic feeling, like I might, just might, have a shot at getting rid of her for keeps. And for fucking his old friend's girl it would serve Glen right to get stuck with the bitch for a few years.

## chuck

So I went out to the store, and after pretending to make some revisions in that week's work schedule (a job that strictly speaking should fall to Walt, my superior, who on the pretext of giving me valuable management experience via delegation has been weaning himself off just about all his own responsibilities over the last couple of years), I stepped onto the loading dock out back and removed from their hiding places five empty, flattened Choos-a-Fed cartons I'd been saving for a while. What kind of a man hides at his workplace empty cardboard cases of Choos-a-Fed, you may wonder? The answer lies in my abandonment some years ago of the drug life. I never, though I was so urged at the time, joined a twelve-step recovery program. Had I joined such a program I would not have encountered Glen in a bar, since participants are honor-bound, as I understand it, to shake off their other addictions as well. Had I joined such a program I would not have spent these last years stewing over Gretchen's fate and plotting different kinds of revenge on Glen. I'll bet I have twenty or thirty such scenarios, of varying degrees of complexity and practicality and lethality.

And now an opportunity had arisen, and I filled each case with what I figured the weight of the Choos-a-Fed would have been, and then I sealed it up carefully enough that it looked brand new and unopened, a level of craft that was probably unnecessary, because he was tweaking like the very dickens when I saw him at the Brass Candle. I loaded the empty cases into the bed of my truck and sat and waited out back by the dumpster.

## torie

So I'm thinking maybe it's time to get out of the hospitality business altogether, once we've made this score up in Topeka, and cut way back on my crank habit before it turns into an addiction.

Also thinking what beautiful babies Glen and I could make, and what a contribution I could make to society after getting my hygienist's license back.

## glen

We're driving north on the turnpike and I am feeling pretty damned fine. This Crumdog will certainly, upon hearing who our mutual friends are, take the Choos-a-Fed off our hands for three, maybe four times what we would have paid poor old Chuck for it. As far as Chuck goes, the cops aren't going to spend much time on the shooting of a well-known low-level pot dealer tossed into a dumpster behind a supermarket. Not the cops I used to know.

As I listen to the female prattling on about our future of domestic bliss, I wonder about leaving her with the bikers. She needs more crank than I can afford to provide, and where I'm going I won't want a woman attached to me at the hip. The turnpike snakes through the Flint Hills, and up around Matfield Green I swear I can feel Frank Sinatra's penis start to vibrate in my pocket out of something not unlike joy.

*Kenji Jasper*

**KENJI JASPER** is the author of four novels, including *Dark,* a *Washington Post* and *New York Times* best seller, and *Snow.* He is also coeditor of *Beats, Rhymes and Life,* a collection of critical essays on hip-hop culture. His writings have appeared in *Newsweek,* the *Village Voice, Essence,* and on National Public Radio. His latest release is *Inter-Course: Moments in Love, Sex and Food.* A native of Washington, D.C., he currently lives in Los Angeles.

# osito
## by kenji jasper

**M**an, you know shit is fucked up when we comin' way the fuck out here," Gary said between puffs. He'd rolled the blunt with a Phillies, which meant it wouldn't last long. I'd told him that there were better brands, but he insisted. "This what I started with. So I'ma stick with these shits till I ain't have lungs no more."

I was never a fan of working high. Hell, I didn't even touch weed or anything else. For me it was all about control, all about making mind and body one whenever needed. But Gary was the one who'd got us the job. So Gary was calling the shots. That's how it was and how it is still, at least in theory. Execution, however, was a completely different matter. At least he wasn't smokin' meth.

"This is where the money is," I said.

Gary's country-fried English made me self-conscious about the way I pronounced my syllables so clearly, a lesson from my father about living in the "other" world, the one where people wore shirts and ties and worried about their balance sheets and annual reviews. All I wanted was a cubicle with my name on it. All I wanted was a quiet place to do my job. Too bad I wasn't any good at it.

"What the fuck does that shit even do?" Gary asked, the blunt already at half.

We'd boosted the car from the Dunn Loring station lot, a white Beamer wagon with factory rims. An '01 or '02 most likely.

But I couldn't be sure in the dark. We were headed to someplace called Osito, about an hour outside of Baltimore. Rico told us it would be like palming a Snickers from a checkout.

My name is Nsilo. Don't ask me where it comes from. I got it from my pops. Any explanation is as gone as he is. He took a .38 slug to the chest on a dance floor six months home from the first Gulf War. All he was trying to do was break up a fight. But when the line on the screen went flat, it was my mama who ended up broken.

Rico had a cousin in Osito, the only child of the only black family in the whole town. This cousin had a father who was on the road most days driving eighteen-wheelers. The mother was the secretary at the all-white Pentecostal church. I could smell the sellout all over them.

"I mean, why in the fuck would you wanna be up and runnin' around all the time?" The roach that remained of the blunt was practically burning his fingers. But he kept pulling from it, even though he was at the wheel a long way from home.

Gary had memorized the directions after a thirty-second read back at the house. A heavy-hitter with a photographic memory is a beautiful thing. As long as you can control him, that is. I'm middle management, which means that I'm the one who takes the dog for his nightly walks.

Much like rap, the crack business ain't what it was twenty years ago. Back in the day, you couldn't walk down a street in the neighborhood without somebody trying to hire you to work one of their corners. But Rockefeller and the Patriot Act and rap changed all of that. That's why Rico got into meth. There's still plenty of money to be made in that game.

So Rico's family of sellouts sold him the location to the biggest meth lab in the county, five trailers in a park of twelve cooking crank like a twenty-four-hour convenience store. We were being sent to make a pickup, one we weren't paying for. There was a bit of other business too. But I was supposed to handle that personally.

When the summer had started I was 100 percent certain that I was headed for the straight and narrow. Meechie had gotten shot outside The Crab House on Georgia Avenue over some broad with more stretch marks than a bag of rubber bands. Our fathers were brothers. My pops had at least made it back from the war. Meechie's had stepped on a land mine. And that was that.

Meechie was the only dude in the world who always had my back. I mean, even when I used to hoop back in high school, he'd be in the bleachers right above the bench, ready to pounce on anybody stupid enough to start a fight with me in it. I was good. But he was better. The game wasn't going to be the same without him.

I had done all right in school. And there was a lady at my church who worked on Capitol Hill. They were short on minorities in the Congressional Page Program. It didn't pay much but she said it was a way into working for the government. I was so fucked up over Meechie being gone that I actually thought it might be for me.

I was used to taking orders and making deliveries. I'd done it all my life. So taking the blue line to Capitol South for the same seemed like a walk in the park. White people were easier to manage than crackheads. Give 'em a smile. Make a joke they understand and you turn into their main boy in a flash. It's even easier when you know how to get 'em what they want. They assigned me to someone named Guy Medscar. He was an assistant to somebody's assistant. But his cousin was a big deal over at the Capitol, a senator I think.

Medscar was one of those dudes who got married out of

high school to a girl who didn't fuck him anymore. He had the four kids, the twin Beamers, the vacation house, all of that. But I could tell that it was more like a life sentence than a week in the Bahamas. My first lesson on the job was that the life everybody wants in the 'hood is a pain in the ass to somebody in the 'burbs.

Then he asked me one day, in a whisper, "You know where I can get some"—his fingers coming to together like they were holding an imaginary pipe—"meth?"

While I had a PhD in crack cocaine, meth wasn't big in my part of town. The way he asked was so funny to me that I thought he was making it up. Meth was for trailer park hillbillies and the fags in Dupont Circle. I might not have known much about it, but I knew where to get it. I knew where to get anything that wasn't nuclear or came with propellers.

"How much you want?" I asked him. His eyes lit up like the Washington Monument after six.

"How much can I get?" he asked.

It seemed simple enough. I went to see the guy sitting on Rico's stash out by Iverson Mall. I brought him a dub that Friday and he gave me a hundred dollars, five times what it was worth. That next Monday he asked me for an eighth. Every three days he'd page me after hours. The code after the number would say how much he wanted.

I hadn't been there two months before I was buying ounces to cover Medscar's orders. Then his boys got in on it. It got to the point where people in the building showed up at his office like it was mine. Since I didn't use (I didn't even drink), the money was all profit.

It really did seem like a foolproof situation. Then the fools got involved.

"So what we supposed to do once we get there?"

"We supposed to holler at this dude named Jeremiah," I explained. "That's all I know."

"You think they gonna have any food up in this jawnt? I ain't had shit since dem wings and fries I had for lunch."

Jeremiah was a prophet. He believed in God so much that he went wherever the Lord told him to go. Sometimes it was places he didn't want to be. Other times it was places he didn't understand. I didn't want to be in Osito on a Friday night.

I had a chocolate star named Deidre sending me pics with her legs open, panties off. She was free for the night. But business was business. This was a run we had to make.

Now, as you might have imagined, it didn't take long for the other pages to see that I was getting special treatment from the boss. I took hour lunches that were supposed to be thirty minutes. I never buttoned the top button on my dress shirt, even though it was policy. And every once in a while, one of my girls would come through.

I made sure my broads knew the deal way before they came over to Capitol Hill. First and foremost, the invitations only went to the right ladies. I couldn't have anybody up in the office who didn't have the sense not to show up in sweatpants with her hair a mess.

Kina was probably my favorite girl. She didn't have much of an ass on her but her hips were lovely, the perfect handles to hold onto while I hit it from the back. She grew up on the block but she had worked at a bank. So she knew how to dress. She came in there one day in a pin-striped skirt and blazer, heels, and a real nice blouse. The blazer was one layer too many in the summer heat, but when she came in the office she was lookin' good, like she always did. Medscar damn near started jerkin' off the minute the girl sat her purse down. I gave him that special nod that explained what I was up to.

"I'm gonna need you to get these supplies for me," he said, making sure to sound really official. Paper-clipped to the list was a key to the supply room. Every floor of the building had one. But only supervisors and the janitor had the key. It was almost as good as booking a room at a motel, without the room service.

He gave me a big wink as I motioned for Kina to follow me out the front and down the hall. I knew he'd studied every inch of the broad, imagining what he might do if her whole world was in his hands. I locked the door behind me once we were inside the room. She lifted her skirt up, flashing the fact that there was nothing between me and her wetness. And that's where I stayed, while hell broke loose all around me.

I had a couple of the other pages making runs for me. I mean, I kept the operation small but I knew beforehand that Meds-car wasn't going to be able to keep his mouth shut for too long. White boys in places like that aren't good at keeping secrets. The ones who can work over at Homeland Security, or at the CIA.

So one of these kids, Jacob, a blond-haired, blue-eyed boy from out in Reston, decided that he was gonna start selling to some of the pages in the other buildings. They had a roll call every morning that he thought was the perfect place to do business. He was in college, after all. Who doesn't get high in college? Instead of selling his usual dimes and dubs, Jacob decided to get a bigger fish on the hook. Some page he'd never seen before pulls him to the side and tells him that he wants to buy a half. The kid, seeing dollars and stars (before the bars), says he can get it. He and Rory, my other guy, had about a half between them. They did the math, but not much else.

The only way to tell that Osito was even there was the lit-up sign at the city limits. The sign was made out of Christmas lights, even though it was just after Labor Day. Beyond it were just the silhouettes of buildings and small moving shadows, most likely raccoons and possums scampering around in the middle of the night. The Monrovia mobile community was about a mile in. The entrance was a concrete apron that led to a dirt road. Gary had to put the high beams on to cut through darkness. The thick dirt road had trailers on either side of it, sleeping souls who would barely remember the sound of our engine as soon as we'd rolled past them. Jeremiah's place was past those, a supersized camper parked beyond the mobile park, right next to a forest.

We were finally there. But I was still back in the supply room.

I can still remember the warmth at the back of Kina's throat; the Snoopy painted on each fingernail looking up at me as she held me tight, her mouth moving forward and backward like a well-oiled machine. She was reminding me of my prom night, and her prom night, and the way her mouth felt just like bona fide pussy when I was inside of it.

My fingers found their way through her (obviously dyed) fire-red hair. Her eyes were closed, like a monk in meditation. I ignored the first fist that came against the door. I was so close to getting *there*. Looking at her, on her knees in front of me, made me wonder what the blowjobs might be like in heaven. I came, just as the door opened, the bullet swallowed by my baby with impeccable technique. It was like a reunion. Jacob and Rory, both in cuffs, Medscar looking like he just got caught with his dick out, and me and Kina with my . . . well, you get the picture.

Jacob and Rory had apparently walked their entire stash right up to an undercover Capitol Hill cop. Of course, they couldn't even get in the squad car without putting me and Medscar's name into it. But as it turned out, the cops only came after me.

I was just another page. He was our supervisor, which gave him deniability. Two white boys selling drugs equaled someone more experienced on the next level up, which equaled me, the black dude from the wrong side of the bridge. The only card I had in my pocket was that it was my word against Jacob and Rory's. In my defense, there wasn't a second out of place on my time card. Plus, there wasn't anyone else to ID me as the top man.

So the worst thing they could do was fire me. I was pretty sad about it, mainly because I'd gotten to like being legit. I liked the check with my name printed on it every other week. But I didn't belong on Capitol Hill (or at least not at that low-ass level). They took my page jacket and my ID and told me that I couldn't come on Capitol grounds again, not even for a tour.

The train ride home was no different than on any other day. I didn't like the way I went out, but I was also looking forward to getting back to Garfield Terrace. Rico always had work there for me. No jackets and ties, no IDs and Capitol cops. There was only one thing I was really good at.

The trailer had one of those cheap locks on the door handle. You know, the kind you can do in ten seconds with some of those little screwdrivers. It was dark inside. The flickering blue light through the outer window was coming from a TV. I was about to knock when the door came open. The man standing there looked like Lil Wayne if Lil Wayne was forty, white, and had a ten-year-old for his tattoo artist. Were the five hairs at the bottom of his chin supposed to be a goatee?

"He must be Gary," the guy mumbled. "I'm Jeremiah."

"How you know *he* ain't Gary?" my driver demanded.

Jeremiah smiled enough for me to see in the dim light. "I just know," he said, welcoming us in.

The chemical smell was everywhere, like those Korean nail shops in the mall. It didn't give me a headache though. Just this dull feeling. I felt like the temperature was dropping a degree at a time. In five minutes I was going to be able to see my breath.

Jeremiah flipped on the light and we saw that we weren't alone. There was a pair of teenaged kids, a girl with dark rumpled hair (and a pair of double Ds) and a white boy with a blond buzz cut and a tattoo of Optimus Prime on his left forearm. They continued to snore like there wasn't a bright light and three people standing over them.

On the other side of the room, a woman old enough to be somebody's great-grandma was asleep in a green recliner that looked older than she was. There was a double-barrel shotgun propped up against the wall behind her, the barrels pointing at the floor.

"So how you wanna do this?" Jeremiah asked.

"We only got a two-seater," Gary shouted. Jeremiah and I both gave him that *Don't wake up the kids* look. Then again, it wasn't like it mattered.

"Where you got it at?" I asked.

"It's back here in the bathroom, brother."

"I ain't your brother," Gary yelled.

Jeremiah chuckled as we started to follow him. "I wasn't talkin' to you, big boy."

There were about five feet between us and the bathroom. I was holding a .380, my favorite piece: light and compact, but accurate as hell. I put my fingers around the grip. 11.85 ounces. Less than a pound.

The tub inside of the bathroom was small. It was the only detail I could make out before the action. Jeremiah's eyes met mine over Gary's shoulder. The stiff-neck movement that was supposed to be a nod was all I needed. There was a single shot before Gary fell forward, his corpse tumbling directly into the tub, as we'd planned. The other players came in from the living room. The old woman and the MTV kids had given the best performances of their criminal careers.

Gary would have said that we deserved "one of those gold things they give for actin'." Comments like those would make it hard for me to actually miss him.

I told you about my cousin Meechie and all that he meant to me. I told you what I went through when that asshole gunned him down in front of the strip club over that broad with more stretch marks than a bag of rubber bands. I just didn't mention that Gary was the one who did the gunning. I volunteered to do the business; Rico and I came up with the plan.

Jeremiah and his crew had gotten on Rico's payroll making D.C. bodies disappear out in the country. The drug shit was just a bonus for them. Those Pentecostal sellouts who gave us the info were Meechie and my cousins. They'd even sponsored us back in the day to keep us out of juvie for a summer or two. They knew DCPD would never think to go body-searching way out in Osito.

Everything I've told you is true, even the meth. Rico is the bank for one of the biggest meth holds in the area. But he knows better than to bring that white-boy shit any closer to the city than it needs to be. I ended up getting back into business with Medscar. But this time he was smart enough to run it all through the boys in the mailroom. My old boss, out of appreciation, pays for my golf lessons at the course uptown.

They say that God has a reason for everything. Maybe that's why I lost that job on the Hill two days before Gary got Meechie. Gary had been my muscle on and off for years. He would have walked anywhere I told him to.

"Anybody else you need to vanish, playboy?" Jeremiah asked, pouring bleach into the bucket of cleanser next to the toilet.

"I'll be in touch," I said.

"What's next?" the ancient woman asked as she leaned

against the wall outside of the bathroom, leaning on that shotgun as her cane.

"I'll let you know the next time I'm through," I said as I started past them. No goodbyes. No last words. It was done.

I could see my breath hanging in the air as I walked through the living room and out the front door. The moon was big and brown in the sky. This was the kind of night where all kinds of things come out of the woods, and out of me. They chase each other in the shadows, a game of chess played up above and down below. The moves almost always come from somewhere else. We're just here on this rock to make the moves.

*Devri Richmond*

**JOSEPH MATTSON** is the author of *Eat Hell* (Narrow Books) and *Empty the Sun* (A Barnacle Book), a novel with soundtrack by Drag City recording artist Six Organs of Admittance. His work has appeared in *Slake, Rattling Wall, Pearl, Ambit,* and more. Mattson was also the literary editor of *Two Letters Collection of Art and Writing Vol. 2* (Narrow Books). His novel, *Courting the Jaguar,* is forthcoming in 2012, and he was awarded a 2011 City of Los Angeles Artist Fellowship for his novel-in-progress, *Hexico.* Mattson lives in Los Angeles.

# amp is the first word in amphetamine
## by joseph mattson

I was awakened at six a.m. after a long night of serious drink chasing down seven days of too much speed. Anvil head, brain ready to splatter, body wrought with ache and despair. Wanting nothing more than some shut-eye, against the ghost-white face of an unforgiving, barbaric narco-crash, I was brought back to the shock of life by a telephone call from an LAPD detective looking for my best friend.

"No," I croaked into the receiver.

"Hello?"

"Yes, hello, yes."

"Is this William O'Sullivan?" His tone had the seriousness of a doctor with very bad news.

"This is he."

"This is Detective Roy Mendoza of the Los Angeles Police Department."

I looked at the clock, the numbers blurry and hopeless. I began to sift through the bitter fog of my consciousness, trying to piece together any broken frames from the grim cinema that had been the past week.

"My lawyer's name is . . ." I said by instinct, but gravity stopped the sentence as I fell headfirst into the closet door, catching the corner of my right eye socket on the knob.

"I'm looking for Jim Grace," he said.

"Jim Grace?" He and I had parted just hours before. But

Grace would take a bullet before doling out my telephone number to the police. My paramount amigo—a true brute hero, rare and holy in the order of what is sacred. Sacred in the sordid world of those who walked our line.

"He's not here," I said.

"I figured. It's just that I can't . . . get through . . . to him."

The way he said it—*get through*—made me nervous. I noticed blood draining from the spot on the side of my face that took the doorknob. "He's not . . . here," I said, adding my own emphasis to see what kind of level Detective Roy Mendoza was on. I'd vicariously become a seasoned veteran in playing blue-boys and criminals, cops and fuck-ups—mostly in the shadow of Jim Grace.

"We tried his phone, but it's a dead end. Perhaps we have the number wrong."

"Look, Jim Grace and I share a mutual distaste for the telephone." I scrounged the floor like a suckerfish, looking for something to compress the wound, the red now rolling down my neck and soaking into my white A-shirt, my face already swollen from the indulgences in modern chemistry, unable to sort out the pain.

"It's in his and your best interest to get back to me. May I give you a few numbers, in the event that you see him?"

"All right, Detective Mendoza, give me the numbers."

"Call me Dozer."

"Dozer. Yeah."

I took off the shirt and clamped it against my eye, stumbling like a drunken, bucking mule through the house until I found a roll of duct tape. I tore off a long piece and wrapped it around my head to hold the makeshift bandage in place. Then I crawled back to bed.

"He's just pissed because I have a pair of his wife's panties."

"What?"

"Yeah. Long story. Another time. Help me with this," Jim Grace said, wrangling a huge yellow tent, trying to stuff it into a little nylon bag. "I'm thinking about taking a trip."

"Good God, you didn't lay a cop's wife?"

"Shit no. Although she is quite a dish. But I hate that bitch. His wife ruined my life."

"Jesus . . ." I mumbled.

"Forget it. I don't have time, nor do I want to explain. Dozer—fuck. He lives perpetually in the past. It's just sad. Two percent?" he asked, handing me a quart bottle of milk.

"Thanks." I grabbed the thing.

"Coat the stomach."

"Grease," I swallowed, "the wheel. Where do you keep them?"

"Keep what?"

"Them. The underwear."

"Underwear?" Grace asked, as if there had been no mention of women's underthings.

"Mrs. Dozer's panties."

"Oh, those. In the freezer."

"Freezer? Why for?"

"Why what? Why not?"

"Keeping a cop's wife's dandies in the freezer is rather creepy."

"You got a better idea how to preserve them?"

"Preserve . . . ?"

"What happened to your face?" Jim Grace asked, as if he'd just noticed it.

"Roy Dozer beat the shit out of me trying to get your phone number," I said. "Why do you need to preserve them?"

Grace lost color in his face, then it returned to its regular bluish flush. "He went to your house?"

I didn't like the way it sounded, in on the kill, same as the cop. Or was I just paranoid, askance from becoming a consistent dope-huffer? Jim Grace was possibly the only person I trusted in this old, bad world. "No, he didn't come to my house. I got coldcocked by the closet doorknob."

"Oh. Put some steak on that thing."

The flashing thought of a cool, thick cow shank slapped against my head, the iron scent of bovine blood and juices sopping my cheeks, dripping slowly down my face, made me feel chilly comfort in addition to horrible nausea.

"Are you coming with me? Jeez, these things. They come in these little yellow bags and once you take them out it is damn near impossible to get them back in." Jim Grace started punching hell into the tent, shoving his foot in, trying his damnedest to make it fit. "You want a Tecate?"

"Yes. What's it for, anyway?"

"Limes are in the fridge."

"What's the tent for?" I asked.

"Pico-Union."

"Pico-Union? You turning vagrant or something? What do you need a tent for to go buy speed?"

"Man, how deep in are you?" he asked.

"How deep in are *you*?"

"Deep? This is just in case," he said.

"Just in case what? In case we wander into the imaginary gnome forest behind the Food 4 Less, or decide to make a nice little home under the freeway overpass?"

"You smartass. It's to throw them off. You never know when the eye is out."

"Well, it's not like we're going to buy crack," I said.

"Man, fighting with doorknobs really fucks up your brain. You're not thinking right at all. We have to expect that they are always looking. We have to be safe, and we need to blend in."

"Blend in? How are we blending in lugging around some huge tent in the middle of the day down in some poor-ass neighborhood with barely any grass to even pitch the stupid thing?"

"That, my friend, is exactly how we blend in. If we were hauling a tent trying to score, say, near the Arroyo hills or Griffith Park or Runyon, we'd be done for. There are reasons to have a tent around those places and we'd be worked over like two-dollar strumpets. But they aren't looking for anybody camping down by Pico-Union. There is no reason for it, precisely why we'll blend in. The obvious becomes the unobvious."

He had me. Drug rationale. Still, it was a little extravagant.

"Still," I said, "it is a little extravagant."

"Bah. Stay here if you want. I'm going to do this thing."


Don't go to Pico-Union.

Not because of the general odds of being caught in gang-war crossfire, or because it's one of the poorest neighborhoods in Los Angeles, policed by the notoriously corrupt Rampart Division, beset by crime and hopelessness, but because the best shit is down there, and by best, I mean worst. The kind of wicked stuff that simulates ecstatic invincibility to its most superlative, supernova echelon—while swiftly as a calculating eagle it grips in its icy talons your heart, your skull, still pumping, pumping and gritting the amp dance, and carries them off for the final sacrifice. Harv holds there. He's a rich mother, playing both sides of the border, he knows the game. He deals two floors subterranean in a squalid slipshod tenement built into a small slope, keeping south of the radar, and also has an estate in the Hollywood Hills, a mile above Franklin. But hell. If you're going to go get drugs, then really go get your drugs. Have some guts about it. Forget the Hollywood Hills. Go to Pico-Union.

Here, you don't have to deal with the crummy debutante princesses hanging around Harv's Hills house, the ones who mistake speed for even more ego and pageantry than they were already bequeathed from their knotty-assholed, smug Black Beauty–gulping Industry parents before them. The cycle, it just does not end. Not only those godforsaken women who drape themselves ridiculously all over the place, but worse, their Chauncey boyfriends who can't even hold their drink, let alone their amphetamine. The only thing worse than people who call the stuff "spizz"—naïve fools who can't come to terms with what they're doing and try to sugarcoat it as if it were kiddy candy, when it is exactly what it is: speed—are the inane, rich parasites who try so hard to be "down" by snorting with the proletarians, when what they really should be spending their easy money and family handouts on is holy pharmaceutically clean Dexedrine and Methedrine, or just go the other way and score some pure pressed opium, or, if they must go up, unadulterated Bolivian cocaine at the very least. Leave me and my drug of choice in peace. For my money—if I had any—I'd stick with the program.

Harv must've been up in the Hills, and Nettles, his skeleton wife, wasn't keeping shop down at Pico-Union, which meant she probably found out that Harv was banging some Westside Debbie back at the ranch. None of his "lieutenants" were there either. Nobody answered. Normally, *someone* is always there.

By this time we'd caught the urge and were facing irate collapse, due to expectation.

"What now?"

"I have to piss," Jim Grace hissed, and stormed off behind the tenement.

I leaned against the building, nauseated by the idea of going up into the Hills, when I heard a fiery "Hallelujah!" burst from the urination.

"Look at this," Grace said, returning. "Perfect."

"Your fly's down."

"Thanks. Okay, so check this out . . ."

Jim Grace had found a nice baggied chunk of ice in his customized underwear—a secret pocket sewn beneath the hangar for his testicles and padded against ball sweat with maxi pads—that he'd forgotten about. We sliced and crushed it even, two fat crystal caterpillars the size of joints, and snorted them behind a dumpster in a trash-ridden alley adjacent to Union. Instantly, my heart jammed itself up into my throat, my eyes blew wide. All dials and switches cranked. The raspy throat of the city screamed like ancient iron daggers against my eardrums and somehow it was sexy, invigorating, a mountainous delight. Compound wizards rewiring the brain to the tune of Armageddon. EVERYTHING GOES UP. I could hear a cricket jerking itself ten miles away. I was locked in.

It was a sun-destroyed four p.m. when we made for the bus. We walked dozens of blocks in swift minutes, the deltas of our chests soaked in long, wide Vs.

"We need your wheels."

"Wheels, yes. And MUSIC. WE NEED MUSIC, NOW!" I yelped.

"NOT SO LOUD," Grace said, loudly.

"Yes, you're right, push the catheter in . . ."

"Catheter?"

"Never mind. We need to get to the number 4 bus if we want the car."

"We can't take the bus all the way," Grace said.

"Into the Hills?"

"Yeah, that was all I had, for sure. We got lucky. I haven't changed my underwear is all. Shit, I'd have washed that chunk later this evening. Lucky, damn lucky."

"Let's get the car," I said.

We made it to the car in good enough time, just before the bus ride from downtown to Hollywood, to my house, might have made my cranium explode. There were bad vibes squaring us from all sides: plump brown mamas hauling bags of groceries and the tender elderly clutching lotto tickets—entirely evil in our peculiar state. Grace and I beyond tense, our innards gnashing at the walls of our skin, probably looking to our fellow passengers like two deranged deviant gimps who'd worked each other into a spastic, primordial lust fury and couldn't wait for some serious fornicating in the privacy of our own home. Or in the tent, perhaps, which Jim was clutching like a bomb whose lit fuse was about to expire. It didn't help that we were constantly whispering gibberish into each other's ears.

After about an hour I located the keys—I'd hidden them from myself during the bad run the week prior—and we were doing fifty on Franklin, feverish for the turnoff up into La-La Land.

"There it is!" Grace screamed over the wail of Neil Young's "Cortez the Killer" spun up to earsplitting decibels.

"I know."

"Man, fuck Cortez!" Grace howled, slapping his knees.

"Look," I said, pointing out the windows at thick chaparral climbing up the rise, houses disappearing into the shadows of oak and rocky crags. "Old Mexico."

"Fuck Spain! Fuck the United States! Goddamn goldbrickers! This is Mexico! Glorious Mexico!" Grace cried, now a hard-wired demon full of fast rage.

"You're not Mexican," I said. I leaned into the left turn going at least 45 mph. After a good fifteen-minute bounce up the mountain we reached the gate and were buzzed in.

"Better leave the tent in the car," I said.

"Right," Jim Grace agreed.

"Gents," Harv greeted us as we walked up the three-hundred-yard stretch from parking to the house. There were about ten cars in the lot, meaning the place was going to be a scene.

"Harv, *que pasa*," Grace said, extending his hand. I simply nodded, keeping my clenched fists in my pockets.

"Come on in. *Mi casa su casa* and all that."

We went into the den—the business room—and as we passed the kitchen I caught a glimpse of Nettles slunk against the stove smoking nothing but two inches of ash from a beaten cigarette. She had a lake of purple around her right eye. I reached up and patted my own bruised orbital plate. When we passed the sliding glass that opened into the courtyard we saw a half-naked blond girl prancing around the pool in a fried haze. She looked no older than sixteen.

"That's Tabby," Harv said. "Her and Nettles are getting . . . acclimated."

In the den Harv measured up two very generous sixties, even though I was just along for the ride; not buying, necessarily, but knowing that Grace would part me off a kind freebie.

"Don't worry about it for now," Harv said. "Two for one today, and you'll make it up to me later."

A loaded deal to be sure. Regardless, Grace and I quickly pocketed our bounties when we heard a gang of intriguing cheers and whistles explode from the clubhouse out beyond the pool. Harv eyed us cautiously, then fixed a stern, secure gaze on us that warned: *You shall not fuck with me.*

"You boys want to come out back and 'tend the ceremony? It's totally cracked."

My throat clenched *no*, but the ill-fated notion sank back down to my gut unspoken. I had a bad feeling. I'd only been up to Harv's Hills house a handful of times, and the place didn't sit right. It always felt appropriate to leave. I'd never seen anything too strange going on outside of meth heaven and hell and their according crimes in general, mostly just a bunch of paroxysmal, self-entitled eccentric turds jettisoning their brains toward sweet oblivion; rather, it was an aura of badness, and all I wanted to do now was go home and read a thick nineteenth-century Russian novel front to back, or masturbate for four or five hours, maybe.

"Ceremony?" Grace asked.

"Yeah. The New Church of Zoom," Harv shrugged. "It's not my thing—pretty fucked-up, really—but they pay me too much to refuse."

We leaned into Harv's taster plate and each took a hefty snort. Somewhere deep down inside not wanting anything more to do with any of this, I still couldn't refuse.

"Well, okay," Grace said.

*Never coming here again*, I swore, *this is the end*, when Harv slid the clubhouse door aside.

"This is Jesus. He died for our—your—sins."

In the middle of the clubhouse stood a meticulously constructed seven-foot crucifix with a beautiful, sleek, powerfully built, but atrociously dead brown-and-white pit bull terrier nailed to it, flies swarming around the bloody spikes driven through its spread front paws and its bundled hind quarters. A male, his eyes expired shuddered in incomprehension. A dozen people were cajoling in a circle, swathed in sweat, caught in the frenzied, possessed grip of fanatical religious conviction. I recognized one of them as an acclaimed actor who'd been in the papers on drug charges, pornography scandal, and spousal abuse. To the right of the sacrificed dog was a much smaller cross with a fanged marmot crudely driven into it, caught sneering in its death. To the left, an empty cross the same size. On a table next to it sat a tray of pulverized methamphetamine, a giant syringe, the necessary means to fire, and a Bible. There were tufts of hair stuck to the bloody rig.

"You're just in time. I guess Judas is next," Harv said, and nodded toward a cage where a handsome white domestic shorthair cat lay apprehensively licking its paw. The dancing freaks of the New Church of Zoom paid us no attention at all.

"Judas wasn't crucified," Jim Grace said. "He killed himself."

My heart sputtered and my gut folded. I have never been one to stomach the slaughter of innocents. I gave Grace a piercing leer, a silent command that it was time to go. He looked pallid, confused, knocked silly from the scene. Before either of us could fully comprehend the massive severity of it: "Now isn't this a surprise," someone cooed from behind, just outside the clubhouse door. I recognized the voice but I couldn't place it. Grace and I turned around and found a thick, sculpted bulldog of a man walking firmly toward us.

"Shit," Grace mumbled.

"What?" I whispered.

"Nothing," Grace said. "Nothing."

The zealots continued, praising the Lord and singing "Blessed All Ye Faithful."

"What the fuck is going on?" I gasped.

The man offered his hand. "Roy Mendoza. Dozer."

It immediately struck me that Detective Dozer was doing absolutely nothing to curb the sacrifice—felony animal cruelty to the highest degree—nor making any attempt to bust Harv or anybody else on enormous drug offenses.

"You've got to be kidding me," I said. I turned to go.

"Give me a minute, Will, please," Grace said.

"Ah, William O'Sullivan," Dozer said.

"You here on a call for domestic aggravated assault?" I asked Dozer, regarding Nettles. Harv hissed a clicked tongue at me and spat on the ground.

"Let's have a seat," Dozer said.

Jim Grace, Dozer, and I sat at a picnic table in the area between the clubhouse and the pool. Dozer faced the New Church of Zoom, and Grace and I faced the house, yet I couldn't help turning my head back to look. The congregation clamored further with song. The detective remained unfazed, and Harv retreated into the angry womb of his manor.

"I haven't heard from you."

"Look, Roy, it's done, man. You can't keep living in the past, right? You've got to move on. I can't do anything more for you. I've gotten on with my life," Jim Grace said.

"Yeah, getting along well, aren't you," Dozer mocked. They talked as old friends gone sour long ago, presently uncertain of what it all amounted to.

"She's gone, man. Gone for good. How many years has it been? Five? Seven? You've got to give up the ghost," Jim Grace said.

"What the hell is going on?" I burst in.

Jim turned, his face wrung with guilt and sympathy, not for Dozer, but for me. "Shit, Will, I'm sorry. I didn't know he was going to be here."

"Just damn good timing," Dozer chimed.

"Roy—Detective Dozer—was on my case, hard, years ago, when I was a driver. Until he discovered his wife was a lesbian.

He found her in bed with Cammy. Strange turn of events."

Cammy—Camille—was Jim Grace's ex-wife. He'd talked to me about her from time to time, how he had not known much true happiness since, and about getting into using afterward, but never exactly why she left. At the time he was a high-paid wheeler for the entertainment industry, escorting celebrities to the most exclusive dealers in town, when heroin was making its comeback in the '90s and speed was mostly for maintenance, and Grace himself had not yet partaken in either.

"They're still together. They divorced us both," Dozer said, his face old and worthless. "Back when I was full of piss and fire," he waved his hand, "and actually cared about all of this. A real star trooper."

I rubbed my temples and dreamed of simpler times, times that I had mistaken for complex, before my own downfall into this exciting, mesmerizing, and delicious and nefarious, dire, and abusive world. I'd been living disenchanted beyond my means for too long, so I thought, just wanting certain kicks—some sort of adjuvant freedom from the pain of life, I guess. But the fee, it seemed, had suddenly grown too large. You cannot blame it on the drug, only the people.

"Speaking of piss," I said, bewildered, disgusted, "excuse me."

I got up from the picnic table, glanced once more at the horrendous scene in the clubhouse, and stormed into the mansion. I went into the bathroom, pulled myself out, but nothing came. I zipped up, flushed the unsoiled toilet, and scrambled through the medicine cabinet for some downers. There were none. I shut the cabinet and looked in the mirror. Alien, a phantom, as if I could no longer place who I was. I produced the sack, crushed the biggest dose I'd ever considered, withdrew a single from my wallet, rolled it tight, and sucked the line dry. I didn't know what else to do. Moreover, at this point I was full of distortion, blasting like a roaring, gnashing, hot-blooded ice comet through outer space. My throbbing, beaten eye could have easily popped with stroke against the mirror. A. Am. Amp.

I walked out of the bathroom and passed Nettles. I paused, turned, and headed into the kitchen.

"What do you make of this shit?" I asked, chewing on my lips, my brain swelling to the palpable limit within the gripping palm of my skull.

"Mind your own business."

"Jesus, Net, you should cook yourself up a sandwich or something. You look like hell. Get strong, don't let the bastard hit you no more."

"I'm getting the fuck out of here," she said quietly. "And I'm taking it all with me."

"Me too. But first I'm going to cook you something to eat."

I feigned rifling through the cupboards for food, secretly contemplating the options of my exit, until I found a large cast-iron skillet that must've weighed ten pounds.

"If I don't ever see you again, for chrissakes, Net, stick up for yourself. You don't need to deal with all this just to get some good crank."

"Why you ain't got no woman, Will?"

"Hell if I know," I said. I walked past her and out toward the pool, the skillet firm in my hand.

Dozer went out like a lit match under tap water. I stood over him panting, having clocked him from behind with all of my might. I dropped the frying pan and scrambled through his clothes until I found what I was looking for. Jim Grace eyeballed the piece.

"What are you doing?"

"Did you give him my phone number?"

"No way. He's a cop, man, it takes him two minutes to figure that stuff out."

"What kind of deal do you have with him, you a selective narc or something?"

"Hell no," Jim Grace shot back, offended by the question. "Can't you tell he doesn't give a shit about the law anymore? He didn't even know we were coming. He was up here doing his own kind of business with Harv."

I almost pointed the thing at him, my best friend. Catching myself, I lowered it. I reached in my pocket for the car keys.

"Go start the car, Jim."

"Dozer just wants the panties."

"Go start the car."

He refused to take the keys. "Be calm, be calm."

"They're killing fucking animals in there!"

"It's none of our business," he said. "I don't agree with it. It's wrong. It's terrible, but . . ."

Jim Grace was holding out because this was sanctuary: a place to connect—any bad, otherwise intolerable sin washed away in the name of screwing-it-on, in the name of assured supply, in the name of, well, addiction, I suppose, or at least undeniable enchantment. The same things that had made me tolerate it all up until now as well. The dose I jammed in the toilet shifted into twentieth gear. The blood in my veins was going for the record, racing like a rocket car across a desert salt flat, reckless and proud, screaming for something official. I turned my back on Jim Grace and stomped toward the clubhouse.

I raised the gun and shot three times into the ceiling. Everyone quivered, turned, stood vacillating before me while drywall and stucco from the bullet holes blanketed the room in softly falling snow. I said nothing, but went over to the cage, opened it, and grabbed the cat by the scruff of its neck and held it close to my chest. Back to the door, I turned and piloted the barrel in a straight line across every one of them. They all stared at me blankly in disbelief—the same look Grace and I had on our own faces when we stumbled upon their terrible ritual—as if I were the one in the wrong. The semifamous, Academy Award–nominated actor moved to speak, but thought better of it. I held fast, my finger microscopically humping the trigger, but I did not bring fire on them. Instead, I honed in on the crucified dog and let a single shot go into its chest, rotated slightly, and too symbolically gave the marmot an honorable death. Then I walked out.

When I returned to the picnic table Grace was shaking. The gun had given him a fever. In the distance, next to the pool, Nettles had Tabby by the hair in one fist, and was burying the young girl's face with the other.

"You coming, Jim?"

"I'm Mexican. By marriage. My uncle. I have a right to care, you know." Grace nodded his head about, regarding the landscape. He had slipped into asylum, unable to deal with the matter at hand.

"Sure," I said. "Old Mexico."

Dozer came to, groaning, the big man curling into a bamboozled little ball.

"Never call my house again," I said. The detective didn't answer. His eyes darted about.

I walked toward the mansion, the cat's claws digging into my shoulder, my ribs. I felt my leg cover in warm wetness. I met Harv coming through the doorway, his face twisted in shock. He saw the gun and moved out of the way. The unmistakable waft of feline ammonia rose from my hip and raided my nostrils.

"What the fuck is going on out here?"

"This is my cat now," I said.

Harv hesitated. He could see it in my eyes: I had gone off to a place where diplomacy was incontrovertible. "Take good care of him," he finally replied.

"His name is Raskolnikov."

"Fine."

"Raskolnikov, you got it? Not Judas, never Judas." I motioned to go, but paused and faced the feared, respected, worshipped pusher. "No more Church of Zoom, Harv. I swear to fucking God, no more. Understand?"

Harv grudgingly nodded his head in false affirmation, with stark ballooning eyeballs full of guaranteed revenge.

"Will," Jim Grace bayed, catching up. "Give me the keys. I'll drive."

I bent sideways, nodding to my front right pocket, not letting go of the cat or the gun. Grace shoved his hand in and fished through my crotch. The episode on the bus flashed in my head. "We're queer," I said. I started laughing, then tears took over, followed by a screaming slideshow in my mind of everything that had just happened—and in the same beat I became quiet, feeling in that moment the terror of cavernous sadness. My eyes dried hard and plateaued on a crux so severe that I was now beyond weeping. We walked down the path.

"How did you get those panties?" I asked.

"I . . ." Grace stammered, struggling not to rush ahead.

"How long have you kept those underwear in your freezer?"

Grace opened the car doors, and the cat, who I'd just named Raskolnikov perhaps for the redemption of us all, trembled on, wheezing against the saturated folds of my sticky shirt. I waited patiently for an answer from Grace, as if our lives weren't in danger; as if there was no reason for concern of the weaponized mob making their way down the path; as if everything up the hill had disappeared; as if we were simply high on a gorgeous meth run; as if the earth itself had frozen and two tight bros had all the time in the world.

M. Abrahams

**JAMES FRANCO** is an acclaimed actor, director, artist, and writer. His film appearances include *127 Hours, Howl, Milk,* and *Pineapple Express.* On television, he starred in the critically acclaimed series *Freaks and Geeks.* Franco has written and directed several short films, and his visual art was featured at Clocktower Gallery in New York. The author of *Palo Alto: Stories,* his writing has appeared in *Esquire,* the *Wall Street Journal,* and *McSweeney's.* Franco has an MFA in creative writing from Brooklyn College, an MFA in fiction writing from Columbia University, and is enrolled in the PhD program in literature at Yale.

# CRYSTAL METH

In my dream I am in Olympic National Park, it is dawn. Moss-draped, shadow-drenched, tortured tree trunks twist upward, reaching for rare sunlight.

I'd never given much thought to how I would die.

Suddenly, in this dream, every creature in the forest is deadly silent. Neither bird, beast, nor insect makes a noise. A predator is near.

Then, in the distance, a tiny snick. I run, fast.

Trees whip past, I dodge branches. I'm chasing something. It's exhilarating. Terrifying. Finally, up ahead, through the whir, the first glimpse of my prey: a deer.

1

JAMES FRANCO: I was asked to write this thing for this magazine about crystal meth and the dangers of it. I didn't know what to write. Then I had this idea: I would write this thing that was like *Twilight* but then wasn't. I mean, I would appropriate the story of *Twilight* but call it *Crystal Meth* and not change anything, and maybe with the new title it would feel different when people read it.

I realized that I couldn't go to the book as a source because the books have been eclipsed

It's running for its life. It darts through the forest maze. It sprints, but I gain. Beyond the deer, I can see the forest's edge, white sunlight glowing against the trees. The deer races for the light. I'm just behind it, about to emerge from the shadowy darkness. The deer leaps into the light in a high arc, it hovers against the white glare of the sun. Then, bam!

It's white and only white all around.

Dying in the place of someone I love seems like a good way to go.

In Arizona, the sunlight. I have alabaster skin, I'm vulnerable. I'm an introverted, imperfect beauty.

I can't bring myself to regret the decision to leave.

Before I left Arizona, I dug up a tiny barrel cactus and put it in a clay pot.

Oh, poor little cactus.

Poor little me.

"Bye, Bella!"

The three tanned, athletic, blond girls

by the films; at least the characters have.

You can never think of Bella Swan without thinking of Kristen Stewart, and you'll always think of Rob Pattinson as Edward Cullen, so I turned to the script, which was easy enough to find online, replete with notes from the writer to change things, such as the buck in the opening dream to a deer. I thought if I just changed the format to prose, took out the scene headings, and put it into past tense, I would get something from my old school waved as they left their McMansion and hopped into a convertible Mercedes. Their flawless, bought-and-paid-for beauty contrasted with my natural paleness.

"Good luck at your new school!"

"Don't forget to write."

"We'll miss you."

I waved back, sweetly, but halfheartedly.

"Have a good . . ."

As I stepped off the curb, I tripped. When I stood, they were gone.

"Life."

Clearly they were not close friends. I have a grown-up demeanor and innate intelligence and their kind is not for me.

Rene, my mom, came out of our house. She's in her mid-thirties. Our house was low-rent for the ritzy neighborhood. Rene is eclectic, scattered, anxious, more like my best friend than my parent. She thrust her cell phone at me.

"It won't work again, baby."

"You put it on hold."

new. It wouldn't be the book, and it wouldn't be the script: it would be a spare and equally bad middle ground that told the same story. I kept thinking about the scene in the biology classroom where Edward gets upset because Bella smells so good he wants to kill her. This, this, I thought, surely this will work, this is addiction, but not just addiction, it is flirting with death, this is the love that kills.

It was difficult to see how I would parse out the desires of the characters and parallel

"I did?"

"Look. You also called Mexico."

Rene pushed me playfully.

We laughed.

"I'll figure it out. You gotta be able to reach me and Phil on the road. I love saying it out loud, me and Phil on the road—woah, *on the road.*"

"Very romantic."

Phil came out. He's good looking with an athlete's body. He held my three suitcases.

"If you call crappy motels, backwater towns, and ballpark hot dogs romantic."

He put his Phoenix Desert Dogs baseball hat on Rene's head and kissed her. Phil's love for Rene is reassuring. Phil headed to the old station wagon to load the luggage, while Rene slipped her arm through mine, clinging to me as we walked to the car.

"Now, you know if you change your mind, I'll race back here from wherever the game is." But her face was strained and I knew what a great sacrifice coming back would be. I forced a smile.

them to crystal meth addiction because I was starting with Bella as the focalizing character and switching to Edward when the addiction element came into play. Then the editor suggested I add some actual parallels between vampires and tweak-ers: never sleep, paleness, sensitive to sunlight, selective diet, one sole hunger, the burdens of living forever.

But I suppose she gets just as addicted to him, in her own way. I mean, he is all she thinks about. And then other things

"I won't change my mind, Mom."

"You might. You've always hated Forks."

"It's not about Forks, it's about Dad. I mean, two weeks a year, we barely know each other."

Rene looked worried.

"Mom, I want to go. I'll be fine."

As she hugged me, I realized I was full of dread, doubt, and regret. I tried to keep the façade up as I climbed into the backseat of the car.

I listened to my iPod, earbuds in my ears, as I got a last glimpse of the sparkling malls, chic shoppers, and manicured cactus gardens.

I said goodbye to the McMansions and goodbye to the scorched landscape baking under the hot sun.

Washington State: nothing but deep, dark, green forests for miles. Lake Crescent. Over it all hangs the mist from the ever-present cloudy gray sky. Everything is wet and green and drenched in shade.

happen. He drives cars really fast, people get killed, and she almost gets raped, and they can't have sex because he is afraid that he will kill her, and blood is always on his mind, and teenagers get killed and kidnapped, and they hide out in hotel rooms from other murderous teenagers, and she is with a hundred-year-old man and she is underage, and then they go to the prom.

It seemed like ALL teenage emotions were there, all wrapped up in a fantastical

The thing about Charlie is that he's a cop. He's taciturn and introverted like me. He drove me in his cruiser down a wet two-lane highway. Trees, drenched and heavy-leaved on both sides. Silence.

"Your hair's longer."

"I cut it since last time I saw you."

"How's—"

"Good . . . it grew out again."

Silence.

"Your mom?"

More silence.

THE CITY OF FORKS WELCOMES YOU. *Pop. 3532.* Logging town. Woodcarvings in the storefronts. Timber Museum's sign: two loggers sawing a stump. Police station: a small wooden building across from city hall, also wooden.

The old house. Two-story, a woodshed full of firewood. A small boat in the garage. Fishing gear, an old buoy. Getting out of the car, I thought: home.

Carried in the bags. The house, not stylish. Only new thing: flat-screen TV. Comfort-

premise, and they—Stephanie Meyers, the filmmakers, and the actors—were getting away with it because it wasn't real, it was just vampires and shit.

Well, I was going to change all that. I was going to show how close meth addiction is to *Twi-* *light.* But then something happened. My manager's partner, Dalton, was hit over the head on New Year's Eve. He was in his front yard, it was nine at night, a nice neighborhood in the Valley out in the Tarzana area, he was walking to his car to go get able, lived-in. Fishing memorabilia; photos of Charlie fishing with Indians. Handmade cards to "Daddy" and photos of me. Me, age seven, in a tutu, sitting stubbornly on the ground.

"I put Grandpa's old desk in your room. And I cleared some shelves in the bathroom."

"That's right. One bathroom."

A photo: a much younger Charlie and Rene, on vacation, beaming with love.

"I'll just put these up in your room—"

"I can do it—" We both reached for the bags, bumped one another. I let Charlie carry them upstairs.

An antique rolltop desk was sitting in the corner. The room was filled with my childhood remnants, which had seen better days. I unpacked my CD case and loneliness finally overwhelmed me. I sat heavily on the edge of the bed, tears threatening . . .

Then we hear a HONK outside. Bella runs across the hall and looks out the window to see—11. OUTSIDE—A FADED RED TRUCK, CIRCA 1960, pulls up . . .        11.

some more champagne for his guests, when he dropped his keys. When he bent over he felt something smash into the back of his head. He fell forward and then stood. No one was around. He quickly called 911 (nine-one-one).

"I think I've been hit by a meteor."

It took the ambulance only three minutes to arrive, despite the meteor comment. They found him sitting on the lawn. His wife and his son, Peter, ran out when they heard the siren.

Fuck shit fuck

EXT. CHARLIE'S HOUSE—DAY

Bella exits to find Charlie greeting the driver, JACOB BLACK, 16, Quileute Indian, amiable, with long black hair, and hints of childish roundness in his face. Charlie and Jacob help Jacob's father, BILLY BLACK (from the photos), into a wheelchair.

CHARLIE: Bella, you remember Billy Bla . . .

. . . zona. Give it up for the rain. And he shakes his wet baseball cap onto Bella's head.

BELLA: xxxxxxxxxxxxxxxxxxxxxxxxxxxxxxxx

She heads toward her seat, brushing off her hair. But she freezes when she sees— Edward. Terrific.

Bella straightens, girding herself. Then strides to the table, and confidently drops her books down, ready to address him. But he looks up at her—          Hello.

EDWARD: Hello.

Bella stops. Stunned. He is direct, precise, as if every word is an effort for him.

8

Peter was the good son, not the older son in jail for possession of marijuana with the intent to sell and possession of an unregistered firearm. That was Sam, the bad son, the son who got some Mexican gang shit tattooed on his boyish Jewish face.

"Please," Dalton had said in the visiting room. "Please just don't get the tattoo on your face, you'll get out and you'll get past this, you can get a job, but don't get the tattoo."

The kid was out and he was crazy and this is what it had

EDWARD: I didn't have a chance to introduce myself last week. My name is Edward
Cullen.

She's too shocked he's talking to her to
answer.

EDWARD (prompting): xxxxxxxxxxxxxxxx
xxxxxxxxxxxxxxxxxxxxxxxxxxxxxxxxxxxx

time . . . as the SUV PEELS out, WIPING
THE FRAME—

107EXT. HIGHWAY, PACIFIC NORTH-
WEST—DAWN107

The sun begins to rise on the empty road
as a sleek, BLACK MERCEDES SEDAN with
tinted windows BLASTS through frame—
108INT. MERCEDES—SAME    108

Jasper driv lic in the passenger seat. Bella
is in the back, her eyes red from crying. She
talks on her cell phone –

BELLA: Mom, it's me again. You must
have let your phone die. Anyway, I'm not
in Forks anymore but I'm okay. I'll explain
when you call . . .

9

he to: His life was fucked
   he blamed his father. He
   to kill his father.
If the ambulance had come
   minutes later Dalton would
   died. They put part of his
   in his abdomen to preserve
hey cut open his forehead

to relieve the pressure beca
the brain had been pushed
ward. There was a hole in
back of his head. The po
were investigating.

   Then I learned that S
wasn't out. He'd be in jai
eighteen more months.

# THE
# END

*Designed by James Franco and Nicole Poor*

# PART III
## METHODOLOGY

Anne Windishar

**JESS WALTER** is the author of five novels, most recently *The Financial Lives of the Poets* (2009), *The Zero,* a 2006 National Book Award finalist, and *Citizen Vince,* winner of the 2005 Edgar Award for Best Novel. His books have been translated into twenty-two languages, and his short fiction, essays, and journalism have appeared in *Playboy, McSweeney's, ESPN The Magazine, Details,* the *Washington Post,* the *Los Angeles Times,* and many others. He lives in Spokane, Washington.

# wheelbarrow kings
**by jess walter**

'm hungry as fuck.

Mitch knows a guy getting rid of a TV. A big-screen supposed to work great. Mitch says he watched UFC on it.

That don't make sense I say. A guy just giving away a bigscreen.

Mitch says the guy has two TVs.

Mitch talks a lot of shit so I won't be surprised if there ain't no TV.

Fish and chips is what I really want. I got twelve dollars which would be plenty for fish and chips. So hungry.

Mitch says it's a heavy-ass TV and we'll need a wheelbarrow for sure.

I ask where the fuck are we supposed to get a wheelbarrow. Like I just carry a wheelbarrow around. Sometimes Mitch.

He says we'll pawn that TV for two hundred easy. Then I could spend my twelve bucks on fish and chips or steak or whatever the fuck I want.

Mitch's sister lives up on the south hill. He says she's got a wheelbarrow. She and her husband garden and shit. I met his sister one time. She seemed cool.

I started loving fish and chips when we had it at middle school. I never had it before that. I used to think chips were the different kind of fries with ridges like we had at school. But it can be any fries.

If we do get two hundred bucks for that TV me and Mitch

are gonna gear up over at Kittlestedt's. On Kittlestedt's icy shit.
Get on a big old spark. None of that scungy east side peanut but-
ter we been bulbing for a month now. Not after we sell that TV.
No more twelve-buck quarters for us.

We gonna amp up on a couple of fat bags Mitch says.

I'm hungry as fuck I say to Mitch.

We gonna eat for days after we sell that TV he says.

He wants to take a bus up the south hill to borrow his sister's
wheelbarrow. Mitch has a bus pass. I got that twelve dollars but
no way I want to spend a buck twenty-five on the bus. Because
you can't even get that east side shit for under twelve. Twelve is
the cheapest I ever seen. Anywhere.

You comin' Mitch asks.

If I do spend some of my money on the bus least I could eat
then. Fish and chips. Or even just get a tacquito at Circle K and
some Sun Chips. I like them Sun Chips too. But I ain't buying
food unless we sell that TV.

Mitch's bus pass is expired. He wants me to pay for both of
us on the bus. Fuck that I say. We get off. The bus drives away.

And I think of something. How the fuck are we gonna get
that wheelbarrow all the way downtown from his sister's house
anyway. It's like two miles. And we'd have to take the wheelbarrow back. Uphill.

Yeah that's true Mitch says.

I known that fucker two years. First time he ever said I was
right.

First time you ever been right Mitch says.

Fuck I'm hungry.

You keep saying that. Fucking buy some food then Mitch
says.

But he knows I can't. I need my twelve bucks. He's just
fucking jealous 'cause he ain't even got enough for a bump.

There's a coffee place downtown where I know this girl. I went to school with her. We walk down there. Keep our eyes open for wheelbarrows. You see wheelbarrows at construction sites sometimes it seems like. But when you need one you sure as fuck don't. I don't think there is a wheelbarrow in all of downtown Spokane.

The coffee shop has outside tables either side of the door. There's two guys in suits and sunglasses drinking iced coffee. They're eating scones. Them fucking scones look great. I'm hungry as shit. The business guys give me a look. Inside the coffee shop I lick my lips to get the salt.

The girl I know ain't working. Sometimes she gives me the day-old pastry. She'll say what happened to you Daryl. And I'll say what happened to you. I forget her name. She's kind of fat now. She wasn't fat in middle school. She was pretty hot I think. But she's fat now.

But that's not what I mean when I say what happened to you. About her being fat. I'm just fucking around. And I did know her name before. I just don't know it now.

Anyways it don't matter because she ain't working. Some guy is working instead. With a goatee. I ask him is the girl who works here around. He makes a face like what girl or maybe he just thinks Mitch and me stink. And he looks at the stain on my T-shirt. I was having a hot dog at the Circle K a few days ago and I was with Todo and that fucker waits until you take a bite of something and then he says the funniest shit. He could be a stand-up comedian Todo. I forget what he said exactly but the ketchup squirted on my shirt. And then it left this stain.

Mitch flops down in a booth.

The goatee guy watches Mitch pick at his face. You have to order something if you're gonna stay here the coffee guy says.

They got these cinnamon rolls must be half frosting. Fuck me I am so fucking hungry. The goatee guy looks at me like I'm a fucking jerk-spazz.

That girl—I have to start over. And then her name comes. Marci! Marci said come in and she'd give me something from the day-olds. Marci. I can't stop blinking.

Marci's not here.

Can you check. Can you check if she left me something from the day-olds.

I am so fucking hungry.

A couple ladies with shopping bags come in.

The goatee dude rubs his head. He leans forward like he's telling me a secret. If I give you tweakers a scone will you get the fuck out of here.

Give us each one.

They got a day-old basket next to the register. The dude takes two scones and gives them to me. One is a triangle. That's the one I want.

Come on Mitch I say.

We go outside. It's funny. Them two business dudes are sitting there eating scones. And Mitch and me are eating scones. Only we didn't pay for ours. Who's the fucking smart guy now.

Only that scone ain't too good. It don't taste like nothing. Not like that cinnamon roll would've. Or like fish and chips. More like wood chips.

Fuck me. I'm even hungrier now.

Mitch and me decide to just walk to the dude with the TV's house. Maybe he's got a wheelbarrow Mitch says.

It's over the river in a big house I never seen before. A covered front porch with a fridge out front. There's like ten people hanging at the house but it ain't a party. Mitch says the dude is strictly into weed but there's a smoked lightbulb on the front porch. I think maybe we'll get hooked up here. But the dude with the TV is all business.

He's eating a Hot Pocket while he talks to us. Fuck me I want that Hot Pocket. So fucking hungry.

You fucking stink this dude says to Mitch.

Yeah I'm gonna go home and get cleaned up after we sell that TV Mitch says.

What's wrong with this guy he asks.

He's just fucking hungry Mitch says.

The dude's got a brand-new TV in the living room. Two little kids are on the PS2. They're playing *Call of Duty*. I'm good on that game I say but they don't look up. The TV is pretty big. How big is that TV I ask.

Fifty-five inch the dude says. He says that's his new TV. The Double Nickel he calls it. The Sammy Hagar.

The picture is too sharp though. It's like sharper than your eyes. That would freak me out. Life ain't that real. On *Call of Duty* I see shit I never knew was there.

The other TV is on the back porch. It ain't even plugged in. It's an old-school projector TV. I worried Mitch was full of shit. But here it is just like he said. This TV is the biggest TV I ever seen. I don't even know how big. The thing's probably five feet tall and five feet wide. Probably three feet thick. It's fucking huge. Like a room. Mitch is right we're gonna need a fucking wheelbarrow.

You want it it's yours says the dude who lives here.

You know anyone who has a wheelbarrow around here Mitch asks the dude.

He looks at Mitch like get your own fucking wheelbarrow.

There's an alley behind the dude's house so Mitch and me go walking along there looking for a wheelbarrow.

I am so fucking hungry. For a while in middle school we got

free lunch. But then my mom worked at the air force base and we got off free lunch. She used to make me cold lunch but whenever there was fish and chips I'd buy my own school lunch. That's how much I liked it. And chili. I liked the chili fine but I really liked them cinnamon rolls. It's funny they always had cinnamon rolls and chili in middle school. I don't know why. They just did.

Fuck. I am so hungry.

I'm gonna kick your ass you don't stop saying that Mitch says.

You can't kick my ass.

A ten-year-old girl could kick your fucking jittery ass.

That girl's six-year-old sister could kick your picker ass.

That girl's newborn baby sister could kick your smelly ass.

That girl's kitten could kick your ass.

That girl's kitten's fleas could kick your ass.

Sometimes Mitch cracks me up. He ain't no Todo but sometimes.

We walk down that alley. There's a kid's Big Wheel. There's a turned-over grocery cart but it's got busted wheels.

And that's when I see it. Hey Mitch look. No shit. Next to a fall-down garage in back of this house. Leaning up against it. It ain't even rusted. A goddamn almost brand-new wheelbarrow. You hear that saying My Lucky Day and I guess sometimes.

There's a little chain-link fence with bent poles. I climb it easy. Grab that wheelbarrow. I wheel it up and heft it over the fence to Mitch. We push that thing back down the alley. We're practically running.

We fucking feel like kings.

I get one-fifty and you get fifty Mitch says. Out of the blue like that.

That's bullshit. I went and got the wheelbarrow.

I knew where the TV was he says.

Don't be a dick Mitch. We both gotta push that thing to the pawn.

One-twenty and eighty.

Don't be a dick.

One-ten ninety.

Fine.

I'm so fucking starving. The TV dude is eating some pretzels out of a bag when we come back. He's standing in his backyard watching his matted dog scoot around on his itchy ass on the dirt. He's laughing like it was a TV show.

The TV dude looks up and sees us. He's surprised we found a wheelbarrow.

How come you don't grow grass back here Mitch asks. That would look better. I can hear in Mitch's voice he thinks we're big shits for getting a wheelbarrow so fast.

I don't suppose you got another one of them Hot Pockets I ask the TV dude.

Nah man. He offers me some pretzels and I take a handful. But they don't taste like nothing. Just the salt.

We leave the wheelbarrow at the bottom of the stairs by the porch and go get on that TV. We can't barely budge it. That fucking TV is the heaviest fucking thing I ever lifted. I can't get under it and once we get it up we drop it.

Be fucking careful Mitch says.

You fucking be careful. You was pushing instead of lifting.

The TV dude just stands there eating his pretzels. Smiling at us. Like he did with the dog with the itchy ass.

Mitch spits on his hands. You got anything else you want to get rid of Mitch asks.

Get the fuck out of here. You guys smell like ass.

We pick it up again. We can't get a hold on it. It's all tippy. But that two hundred bucks is out there so we muscle it down the steps. It don't go in the wheelbarrow very well. Kind of sits on top on the rim. And it weighs so much it flattens the wheel. Fucking brand-new wheelbarrow and the wheel goes almost totally flat.

Fuck Mitch says. You got a pump man.

Get the fuck out of here the TV dude says. Fuckin' chalkers.

So we push it down the alley and then down the street. I'm on the front of the TV keeping it steady. Mitch is holding the wood handles of the wheelbarrow and pushing. We go really slow like that. A few feet for a minute and then we got to stop. It would be easier if the wheel had more air. But it still wouldn't be easy. I'm sweating. The sweat keeps getting in my eyes.

Fuck Mitch says.

I know I say.

I'm balancing that TV and walking backward. One time Mitch trips a little and the TV starts to go over and I just get in front of it. I just keep it from going over. Motherfucker watch what you're doing I say.

Sorry Mitch says. I tripped. He gets on the TV too and we get it balanced again.

It's six blocks to the pawn. It probably takes us ten minutes to go a block. Some kids are riding bikes like sharks around us. They stop to watch. One of them is eating a sandwich.

Mitch has to stop to wipe his sweat and breathe. I'm crazy fucking hungry.

What kind of sandwich is that I ask the little kid. It looks like cheese but not with the cheese melted just slices of cheese on white bread.

Fuck off tweaker the kid says. And he rides away on his bike eating that cheese sandwich. Or whatever kind of sandwich it is.

I swear if I wasn't on this TV I would pull that kid off his fucking bike and beat his ass. We didn't talk to older guys like that when I was a kid.

The next block goes a little faster. I think of that girl at the coffee shop and I wonder if she gives me the day-olds so I'll leave like the goatee guy did. But I don't think so. I think she likes to talk to me.

She gave me a cinnamon roll one time. That's how I know they're so good there. Remember these in middle school I asked her but she didn't remember the cinnamon rolls. Anyways that cinnamon roll was sure better than them dry scones. I wonder why them businessmen would eat scones when they could afford cinnamon rolls or even oat bars or muffins. I wonder why the fuck they make scones in the first place.

Why the fuck you think they make scones at all I ask Mitch.

Great mystery Mitch says.

Sometimes he is as funny as Todo.

The third block goes even slower. Mitch's arms are shaking. Red splotchy covered with sweat. And I feel dizzy from all the walking backward. You gotta switch me Mitch says.

So I push for a few blocks and Mitch steadies. Only I don't trust his steadying so I push more carefully than he did. It yanks your arms out of their sockets pushing that wheelbarrow. And even though it's a pretty new wheelbarrow I get a sliver from the wood handles.

Fuck me I say. I got a sliver.

I got like a hundred.

You got a hundred slivers.

I said LIKE a hundred.

We get four blocks. Only two to go. We stop at this yard and take turns steadying while the other guy rests in the grass until this old guy comes out and yells get the fuck off my yard. I'm gonna call the cops.

Fucking call 'em then Mitch says.

Where'd you steal that TV the old guy says. He's waving something at us.

Fuck you Mitch says.

But for some reason I don't want the guy to think we stole it. We got it from a guy I say. And the wheelbarrow. Even though we didn't get that from a guy but stole it.

We start going again.

And I think of something. The old guy had a remote control. I say that to Mitch. You see that. I just thought of it. He was waving something at us and it was a fucking remote control.

Yeah Mitch says and we both laugh. Fucking people Mitch says.

Like a sword I say. He carries that remote around.

People spend their whole lives in front of that fucking box says Mitch. He says it like we got the life or something.

We're a few houses away from Monroe. The busy street with the pawn.

There's a Hawaiian grill place on Monroe just down from the pawn. They got this chicken and rice but it's at least five bucks. That sounds even better than fish and chips. That would leave me with just seven bucks though. Can't get no bump for seven bucks.

I think I'm gonna fucking starve to death Mitch. I'm dying here.

We're almost there he says.

Fucking kings.

By the time we get to the last block the whole tire has gone flat on the wheelbarrow. Now I'm just pushing on the steel rim. It's like pushing a fucking house uphill.

Pull motherfucker.

I am.

We can barely get it up on the sidewalk and then there's a curb cut and we can barely get up the other side of that. My hands are red raw. I been pushing the last three blocks. I should get half I say.

Fine Mitch says.

At the pawn I stay outside and steady the TV while Mitch goes inside. Some dude is coming out as Mitch goes in. He just bought a circular saw. He laughs at me. That's the funniest thing I ever saw he says. Fucking tweaker standing with a giant old TV on a wheelbarrow. And he takes out his phone and takes a picture of me.

I don't care. I just smile for the picture. 'Cause we made it. Fuck the TV dude and the little kid with the sandwich and that old guy with the remote and this guy with the camera phone. My big problem now is whether to have fish and chips or that Hawaiian chicken and rice.

The pawn guy comes out with a big-ass grin on his face. He stares at that TV like he can't believe we pushed it all the way there. It is pretty fucking cool now that I think about it. All the shit we went through. Fucking day this was.

How far did you guys push this thing.

A mile Mitch says.

This kind of pisses me off. It's enough what we done without making up some story. Six blocks I say.

No shit. And he shakes his head like we come from the North Pole or something.

It works great Mitch says. I just watched UFC on it this morning.

That pawn dude has the biggest grin on. Follow me he says.

I don't want to leave it here I say. It might fall.

The pawn dude helps us lean it against the wall of the store.

Then he takes us inside to where there's ten TVs hanging

up. Most of them are flat and big like that TV dude's new double nickel. They're all plugged in. They all work good. Them new TVs are like two hundred bucks is all.

You guys see any big-console projection-screen TVs in here. We say we don't.

No transistor radios or VHS players either. You guys are like five years late. I couldn't GIVE that fucking dinosaur away. I couldn't give it away if it came with a free car and a blowjob. Now get it the fuck out of my store.

In front of the pawn Mitch and I got nothing to say. We just stare at each other. Mitch looks sorry. He probably thinks I blame him. But I don't. Fuck he didn't know. It was a good try. A lot of things are like that. Good tries. I just wish I wasn't so fucking hungry. And I wish I had enough for Mitch's bump too and for some fish and chips. But I don't. I just got the twelve bucks. Mitch knows. He looks like he's gonna die. Pale as shit.

I tell you what. We look back. The pawn dude is standing there. He's been watching us. I'll give you ten bucks for the wheelbarrow.

Fifteen Mitch says.

It's got a flat fucking tire the guy says. But he smiles. Like he's watching that dog rub its ass. Okay he says. Fifteen.

You gotta take the TV too I say.

What am I the fucking United Way here the pawn guy says. Fine. Take it round back and put it in the alley. So we lift it again off the wheelbarrow. It's like needles in my back every step we take with that fucking TV. My face is pressed against the black console which is a thousand degrees from the sun. My hands are so sweaty I'm sure I'm gonna drop it. But we make it to the alley where we leave it with a bunch of other garbage. Wire. Old shopping carts. An axle.

The guy gives Mitch fifteen bucks. You guys know I'm doing you a favor he says. I'm not gonna get fifteen bucks for that wheelbarrow. You know that right.

Yeah we say.

Good he says. Then since I'm doing you a favor you can do me one. Next time you cat shit—smelling motherfuckers get some idea to steal something and pawn it you go to a different fucking store, right. Go to Double Eagle over on Division. Fuckin' chalkers the pawn dude says.

Mitch goes to give me half of the fifteen but I say that's okay. We each got twelve bucks now. Plus three left over. We ain't making it to Kittlestedt's but that's okay. We'll go over to the east side where a fucker can still be king for twelve.

And that leaves us three bucks to eat on. It ain't enough for no fucking fish and chips. But we got enough for the Circle K.

Kings.

Mitch gets a pepperoni stick. I get a ninety-nine-cent big bag of Sun Chips. And we split a Dr. Pepper. The clerk wrinkles his nose but fuck him.

Then Mitch and me start walking toward the east side. I wish I would have thought to ask that coffee shop guy when that girl works again. The one who I went to middle school with. Fuck me. I think I forgot her name again.

I can't even taste the fucking Sun Chips. It's like they got no taste at all.

Then Mitch starts telling the whole story. Remember that free scone you got us.

Like I wasn't even there. Yeah I say.

And you saw that fucking wheelbarrow like you blew out your birthday candles and wished for it.

I laugh at that. Yeah.

And we come back and that fucking dog is scooting on his ass.

And even though I was there for all of it I laugh at every fucking thing he tells me about our day. We walk and Mitch tells the whole fucking story again. I think he's gonna tell that story forever. And I didn't laugh once when we were doing that shit. But now it all seems so fucking funny I can't hardly stand it.

I guess remembering is better than living.

And what about that dude waving his remote control Mitch says.

Yeah what the fuck was that.

Maybe he was a fucking Jedi knight Mitch says and we gotta stop walking we're laughing so hard. Fucking Ben Kenobi I say. And we both bend over laughing. And fuck me it's nice to be out walking. To have twelve bucks in your pocket and some tasteless Sun Chips in your belly. We walk and we laugh. All the way over to the east side.

*Amy Sullivan*

BETH LISICK is the author of four books, including the *New York Times* best seller *Everybody into the Pool*. She is also an actor, filmmaker, and the cofounder of San Francisco's Porchlight Storytelling Series.

# tips 'n' things by elayne
## by beth lisick

*12/20, 7:36 a.m. Audio Recording #1*
The appetizers are going to be easy-peasy because all I have to do is do what I did last year, except be a little bit more on top of things during the actual party, and then we'll see how blown away everyone is. That, and the addition of the hot pots, is really going to take it to a new level. Fondue, anyone? Who says you have to call the Tasteful Affair catering truck just to have a holiday open house? You know who you are. Just because you have money doesn't mean you can do it better by hiring someone. Fuck you, Tammy, and the horse you rode in on whose name is Jacob Martinson, a baloney of a realtor.

Are you still with me? Why, hello, listeners. Let's start over. First let me say that doing this recording was Jim's idea. I'm one of those people who always gets asked, *How do you do it?* My friends literally stand there with their hands on their hips, just shaking their heads, laughing, saying, *How do you do it all so effortlessly, Elayne? And with such verve and zest and appeal and aplomb?* And, you know, there I am with all my balls in the air and I'm wheeling around on my unicycle, blindfolded, saying, *What? What are you talking about? I'm just being me!* So Jim says, *Honey, just strap the recorder on while you're getting ready for the party as a kind of experiment. It'll be interesting,* he says. *A testament, of sorts.* Our oral histories are more important than ever. So this is for anyone who wants to know how I do it all, or maybe even for you, Sasha, if my entertaining gene ever kicks in and you decide you want to take my advice for a change. For the record, I have not seen Sasha since last night at six when she went over to her friend's house to supposedly study for the SATs. Ho ho ho, says Santa to the child. Naughty or nice, babygirl? Just answer me that one. Naughty or nice.

Okay, moving on to the official business. My day. First things first, when the feet hit the floor, is doing my tape. Before coffee or grapefruit or brushing the fuzz from my tongue, I get my exercise. I'm going to turn the recorder off while I pop my routine in the VCR and start sweating. Jim says this thing is voice-activated, that during the boring parts it'll go off, but I don't trust it yet. For the record, I do the tape five times a week, not just when I have an event. That, plus a daily walk with Galileo the Wondermutt, and my backside looks as good as it did the day I graduated from the conservatory. Goodbye.

*12/20, 8:25 a.m. Audio Recording #2*

Mi, mi, mi, mi! I'm baaaaaaack. And a little winded, as you can tell. I never had asthma or anything, but sometimes I think all those backstage cigarettes I sucked down in my twenties are coming back to haunt me. I may have subpar lung capacity, but can you do this? If you stick a stock of liquor in your locker, it is slick to put a lock upon your stock, or some joker who is quicker's gonna trick you of your liquor if you fail to lock your liquor with a lock. Ha! That, my friends, was my favorite tongue twister from ye olde thespian days. I got a million of 'em! You need unique New York. Hoo. Let me catch my . . . [*sound of Elayne's breathing here, a wheeze is detected*]. Oh, brother. And don't smoke, everybody. Oh, great. Now what am I doing? A public service announcement? Next thing you know, I'll be telling you how to perform the Heimlich, which actually did save my life one time, but that's a story for another day. And it's definitely rated R for raunchy because I was nude. Excuse me! Let's get down to it.

Oh, there's Jim turning off the shower. Jim! Now, on the invitations I said the party was from four p.m. to eleven p.m. in order to give everybody a window in which they could attend. Even the Tagmeyers, who are always booked-up, are coming. Last year, we didn't start till six and I really felt that for some of the older folks in the neighborhood it would be nice to get things started while it's still light outside. Make some hay.

I don't know what I did before the island. Seriously. My hand before God, as I stand here in the kitchen, before we remodeled I didn't have this gorgeous island with the Corian countertop to sit and have my coffee at every morning. It's so smooth and durable. I could run my palm across it all day long. That, and the new automatic espresso machine that tamps the grounds down and has a self-frother, really make my mornings feel like they are straight out of a TV commercial. Or a TV show even. A program.

Oh, here comes Jim! Big Jim. Give me a kiss, honey. Big man go to work and win bread for family. I love you, big man! Jim, say hi to the recorder.

*Uh, hello recorder.*

I'm doing the thing you said. Breaking down my party-day schedule for people who want to be in the know.

*Oh great, honey. I've always said you were a magician.*

Tell the good people what a magician I am!

*This woman is a magician!*

I am. I feel great. I feel super-great.

*Okay. I'm working a half and then I'll go to the deli on my way home and pick up the stuff.*

And the special mustard.

*And the special mustard.*

Honey, do you ever breathe in and feel like someone put your oxygen on ice?

*Hmm?*

Nothing. Just get out of here, you big galoot. There he goes. That was my prince, my number one fan.

Okay, next thing we're going to do is get out the old stone tablet and chisel our list of all the dishes that are going to be part of the big holiday smorgasbord. Here we go. Fondue. Check. Potato torta. Deviled eggs. Classic. Spare ribs and dip. Black bean dip. Side of tortilla strips with those. Peanut and dill dips with roasted veggies. Having roasted veggies as opposed to raw is so much classier, I think. Focaccia and tapenade. Crab and artichoke dip, which is so cheesy and good. Dates and Parmesan. Jumbo shrimp—gotta love that oxymoron—and cocktail sauce. Mini quiches. Throw 'em in the oven. Easy. Curried phyllo triangles. Always a winner. Nuts. Mediterranean meatballs. Baked brie with pear and cranberry preserves. Salmon with my special orange miso sauce.

There. Mouth watering yet? And we haven't even gotten to the dessert buffet. Hold onto your hips! I've made chocolate truffles and Rice Krispies treats and cookies with broken candy cane pieces on top, and of course we have Linzer torte. And Jeannette is bringing the strudel when she comes over. Now, I'm going to put this list up on the fridge, so I can easily refer to it. There's a tip for you. And let's go pull my dress out of the guest room closet and take the plastic off to air it out. Size four, fits better than ever. Red satin. Satin Doll. The Lady in Red. I heard a terrible story on the radio about how toxic dry-cleaning is, but I have to say, there are certain stains that definitely need to be removed by chemicals. And get your mind out of the gutter on that one because I am referring to a thick, creamy white substance called . . . Miracle Whip. What do you think of Dijonaisse? I don't like it, thank you for asking.

You know what? This is actually fun, talking to nobody and

everybody all at once. It makes me feel free somehow. A creative outlet for a gal who's always liked to let it all hang out. There's been a little lull since closing night of *The Dinner Party*. I don't know how many of you saw me reprise my role as Yvonne. That was a blast, as anything by Neil Simon always is, but it's good to have a project like this to keep my juices flowing before the next audition. Rick says they're talking about doing Durang's *Beyond Therapy* in the fall. Total laugh riot! We shall see, we shall see.

Next thing we're going to do is hop in the Cube and take care of a few last-minute errands. I love that car. Why not be fun? Now, there are certain things that you have to do on the day of the party. Flowers, for one. I'm sure I'll end up receiving a few bouquets from my minions, but it's good to lay down a floral foundation, so to speak. I can see here as I pull away that Mr. Paco did an amazing job on the yard yesterday. He is not your typical blow-and-go gardener, so if anyone wants a referral, I'll get you in touch with my man Paco and his sons. I hate this speed bump.

Oh, just go. GO! Jesus fuck, could you learn the rules of the road? The zipper effect! Learn it! Never any parking down here anymore. My turn, my turn! Oh, those trees are cute. They put little packages underneath them. What? Are you kidding me? Kip's is supposed to be open by now and it's not. All right, people of the planet, who exactly has the spare time to sit in the car for ten minutes while this woman diddles around in the back heating up her oatmeal packet in the microwave or whatever she's doing while there are customers here? I'll be right back.

*12/20, 10:06 a.m. Audio Recording #3*
Done and done. Tuberoses are sent from heaven. I thought she was going to try and overcharge me like she did last time, but

apparently I made an impression. Now off to get the ice. Uh-oh. Phone call!

Sasha! I have you on the Bluetooth!

*What time do I have to be home?*

Well, hello, wonderful daughter. Good morning and hello. The party starts at five, but you should come home early to get pretty and help me out. And you have your appointment at 2:30.

*I don't know what you're talking about.*

Your weekly appointment.

*Oh. I'm not going.*

Of course you are. I'm out and about, so I could pick you up right now if you want, okay? Hello? Hello? Can you hear me? Sasha? Oy! Sasha!

Fifty shekels and a crêpe suzette to anyone who can solve this teenage epidemic of attention deficit and nihilism running roughshod through our society right now. At least when we were young, we used to care about something. Green means go, Lexus. Pick it up!

New topic. Kids . . . This is my radio announcer's voice, by the way, back when I did voice-over. Kids, have you ever been to a party that ran out of ice? Major bummer! Or how about when the hostess uses oniony ice from her funky old ice cube trays? Boo! Hiss! We definitely don't want that, so make sure to stop by Silver Liquor and pick up three ten-pound bags of ice for your party. You'll be glad you did!

The last thing we have to do—oh there's Linda Hakido. Linda! Linda! You're coming, right? Don't forget your dancing shoes!

You should have seen her husband last year. A real party animal.

All right, we need to stop and get a couple more cans of crabmeat because now I'm remembering how fast that dip went last year. Come with me into the singular oasis that is Food Town. You think it's going to be a crap store from the outside, but they carry almost everything I ever need except for my brand of tampons.

*12/20, 10:42 a.m. Audio Recording #4*

Mohammed! I need more crab in the can! I'm having my big shindig tonight and the natives are restless. And hungry! [*Mumbling*] Well, yes. Yes, you are cordially invited, Mohammed. Of course you are. [*Mumbling*] Oh, I thought you were serious! Okay, then. Happy holidays.

Whew, sheesh. He had me going there for a minute. He did. Not that I wouldn't have him in my house, but I barely know him. We're already packed to the rafters with real friends, which might be a good topic for a separate installment. Who to invite and why? Inquiring minds. Let's get Jim on the horn.

*Jim Whiting, manservant!*

Stop it! I just want you to remember the dark mustard.

*I'm remembering the dark mustard!*

Great. I've already got the flowers and the ice and more crabmeat and I'm heading back, pronto.

*You're not getting wound up, are you?*

No, except for Sasha who's pulling a disappearing act.

*Okay, remember to stay calm and everything's going to be fine.*

Ciao, honey.

*Ciao.*

*12/20, Noon. Audio Recording #5*

Home again, home again, jiggity jig. I'll put the ice in the garage freezer and get the flowers in their vases and get on to the rest of the food prep while I have my smoothie. First I get all the veggie chopping out of the way, then I grate the cheeses and get the eggs boiling. I know you can't see me right now, but I feel as if I'm moving like a panther. Can you see me, God? Am I moving like a panther? Like, right now, as I go from cupboard to fridge to microwave to pantry to chopping block. What kind of cat am I? I want answers, and here are the meatballs nestled in their Tupperware right where I left them.

[*The stereo plays Van Morrison's greatest hits while chopping and various other kitchen noises are heard. Elayne sings along, most exuberantly to "Brown Eyed Girl," which she replays three times in a row, getting louder and more into it each time. A muffled sound that could be crying is briefly heard. Elayne blows her nose.*]

Some people find food prep boring, but I find it meditative. Let's go make sure all the chafing dishes and serving platters are where I need them and then I'm going to talk to you all about something very important. Are you ready? Galileo, you're a good doggie. So handsome. Okay. Here goes: I always feared the Taj Mahal would look like a giant biscuit box! I repeat, I always feared the Taj Mahal would look like a giant biscuit box! That's the genius of Christopher Durang, and if I don't get the part of Prudence, some little fagalag is going to be strung up by his balls. Of course we know I'm talking about Walker, who is one of my closest friends, even though he has no tact. Watch him take over the piano from Jim tonight. Just you wait!

Living room? Spectacular. There is not a mote of dust to be found after yesterday's white tornado, and I've got my bar stocked with everything you could imagine, plus I am doing a special seasonal drink. There are even a couple Santa hats there in a basket because I thought it would be cute for people to wear them when they take turns behind the bar.

Now, we shower. Don't look, recording device! I'm going to expose myself.

*12/20, 3:13 p.m. Audio Recording #6*

Oh, that's better. Lying down for just a minute to gather my strength. Oh, forget about it. I've got things to do.

Slide into this hot little number. Like a glove, I tell you. I'm doing my hair in a messy bun. There was a gal in the Rush Street Players who used to do this style and I think we've got similarly shaped heads and it just works. You want something loose and casual when you are rocking a dress this sexy, that's for certain. To pantyhose or not to pantyhose? That is the question!

Oh boy. This is important. One of the last things I do after I reward myself with a pre-party vodka is step outside the front door. Then I walk in as if I am a guest in my own home. Let's do it together.

Hmmm. What do we see? Where is my eye drawn? For instance, look at Sasha's ponytail holder sitting right next to little Kris Kringle. That's not very tidy, is it? Or look how the poinsettias are just slightly off-center on the mantle. I tell you, so much of this is in the eye. I'm not sure that it can be taught, the way that I see, but hopefully you're getting something out of this. I know I am! There's Jim opening the garage. Jim! How's the deli tray look?

*It smells great in here!*

How are my cold cuts looking? I'm about to fire up the hot pots and get the fondue going. I decided I am like some kind of cat. A wildcat!

*Are you okay? Your cheeks are flushed.*

Don't let Walker kick you off the piano so quickly this year!

*I'm going to take a shower.*

I'm in the middle of my recording.

So call me crazy for this next one, but I feel like the bathroom is a very important place to be thorough. Think about it: a fabulous open house in a charming and well-appointed home at the height of the frenetic holiday season. It's the kind of home you pass when you're out for your evening constitutional and think, *I wonder who lives there. That sure does look like a warm and inviting place to live. Some very creative, lovely people must be inside right now doing something interesting.* And suddenly, you're there! In the middle of the whirl and swirl of guests and chatter and activity and carols around the baby grand and then, boom, you've got to tinkle and/or check your lipstick. When you do, I want you to say hello to your own little sanctuary.

I like a scented candle. I like to play with lighting. I like to do my towels two ways. Plush, vibrant terry ones, of course, but also a high-quality disposable for those who would rather take that route. I'm not judging. The main goal is to make everyone feel comfortable. Now, how do I put this delicately? Because I'm taking this warts-and-all approach, let's get past the bullshit. I want to point out that it is advisable to take a quick peek inside the medicine cabinet and get a gander. Whether you'd like to admit it or not, some people, and I'm not going to call them cretins—though I'm sure Tammy Two-Tone, who gets that special name because of her horrible hairstyle—are bound to check out what's cooking inside the cupboards. Generally, the only things I relocate to my dresser drawers are Jim's fungal powder and any prescription medications that may be around. Am I right? You don't want every Tom, Dick, and Harry, and TAMMY, knowing who's on what for why.

Did you hear that? I think it was a knock at the door. Here we go scurrying down the hall, slipping into the red patent-leather pumps on the way there. Goodbye! This has been fun! Showtime!

*12/20, 4:02 p.m. Audio Recording #7*
Oops. My bad. I thought I heard something. No guests yet, but

I am going to turn you off anyway because I still have to make the mix for the pomtinis. So perfect that pomegranate juice is red this time of year. That doesn't make sense, but you know what I mean. I couldn't resist. This is amazing. This is my night.

Rose Bunch

**ROSE BUNCH'S** fiction and nonfiction has appeared in *Tin House, New Letters, Gulf Coast, River Styx, Fugue,* the *Greensboro Review,* and *PMS poemmemoirstory.* Winner of a 2010 *New Letters* Dorothy Churchill Cappon Prize for the Essay, a Pushcart Prize nominee, and third-prize winner of the *Playboy* Fiction Contest, she received her MFA from the University of Montana and a PhD from Florida State University. As a Fulbright Full Grant Scholar to Indonesia, she spent the 2010/11 academic year living in Bali, and is now completing a novel set in her homeland, the Arkansas Ozarks.

# pissing in perpetuity
## by rose bunch

never saw the coons that ate my koi. At least, I never saw them do the eating. What I saw Sunday morning as I lay belly-flat on the mossy river stones surrounding the hole me and John dug, lined with black tarp from Lowe's, was empty, clear water. The only movement a rippling from my water feature: a serene, concrete woman constantly pouring from an urn cradled against her naked breast. I nicknamed her "Lola" because she had a mannish jaw. "It sounds like someone taking a perpetual piss in our backyard," John said when I first plugged Lola in. I got up, poked around, and saw the coons had left behind tail bits—a fin here, a scale or two there. I imagined them washing their nimble, little hands in the empty pool at my feet. Lip-licking satisfied.

"Goddamnit," I said, and felt myself welling up a little bit, about to squirt like Lola. I named the fish after two of my favorite dead uncles, which was shortsighted of me if Winfred and Ransom had to be buried all over again should the aeration pump break down or coons come for blood. I fingered the golden flakes of their remnants and sprinkled them back into the water. A partial sea burial.

I now saw Butterball next door, watching me, pissing in my general direction. A stream of urine shooting from a small pink knob of flesh pinched between his fingers. He had lost a ton of weight in the past few months, but his frame still looked built to hang meat on, lanky and misshapen even for a teenager, with hunks of clinging lard deposits. He removed a cigarette slowly from his lips, ashed, and shook his dick, eyeballing me from behind reflective Bassmaster shades.

This was a hill trick I knew from childhood: don't stand and stare, but don't be the one to look away too quick either. A glancing square-off. From inside the old stone house behind him I could hear the keening wails of his younger brother, a six-year-old. Their mother's car was gone again, and when she was away the boys often spent too much time in their yard, worn bald by a chained dog, staring at ours. The six-year-old played in the dirt and a growing junk pile, while the former fat kid paced back and forth talking on his cell phone and smoking cigarettes, out of reach of the skinny Rottweiler pressing full chain for affection. He flicked the butts toward our house, and I had to police the yard to pick up the ones that made it across the border. I washed my hands immediately, because they had grazed what he had suckled.

I wondered what they ate when the mother was gone for long, up to several days by my count. What the inside of that house must have looked like, the darkness and stink of it. Some days I thought I could literally smell a stink coming off it, and I wondered what they did inside there, what poison they might have taken or produced.

"They seem too stupid and disorganized to be cooking," John would say whenever I brought this up. "Taking, but not cooking."

"You think it takes real smarts to cook meth?" I would say back. And we would watch on the news the ugliness unfolding night after night in the hills surrounding us, the broken and blank-eyed faces in mug shots and wailing, filthy children taken by child protective services.

My mother used to bring me to the homes of the needy families when I was a kid. We delivered donated clothes or canned goods from the church to people up in the remote hollows who squirreled their lives into whatever passed for a house. Velveteen couches and cigarette-charred La-Z-Boys, collections of Avon perfume bottles on every surface, plastic flapping on windows. They were grateful for the canned peas, the used coats, the fresh pears from our tree. Old, isolated communities in these Ozark hills were once sustained on this type of charity. They were just poor, either by bad luck or accident, but that wasn't a crime. Lots of people were poor then. It didn't mean they had to be assholes too.

Three months ago, Butterball and family had moved into the house that the realtor claimed was condemned when he sold us our land. The houses we could afford in town were all on small lots in cow pastures out by the interstate. No sidewalks or trees. No privacy from your neighbors who were close enough to piss on. No charm either in any of them advertised as such, their gold-flecked linoleum and taupe-carpeted floors felt as dull and cheap as the interior of a shoebox. We constructed our own charm then. Here in Wesley, Butterball and family were the only neighbors close enough to holler at, and the next home over was a bunch of Guatemalans in an old trailer who worked the chicken trade and kept to themselves. I'd suspected the Guatemalans of dealing because of the traffic coming and going at the trailer, but when I called the sheriff's office a tired-sounding woman said, "Honey, they'll see if they can get around to it." Later I thought maybe all the traffic was partly because there were so many of them living there, but nobody ever came out to check. I called the sheriff again and the same woman said: "No telling what they're up to, we got so much of that we can't keep up. Whatever it is, they'll probably stick to themselves." If they weren't going to do anything I was glad nobody had pulled up in a squad car mentioning drug-trafficking complaints from the nosy white lady up the road. Still, I watched them closely looking for signs. The men, and a few women, drove past packed in an old Dodge every morning and night, a steady rotation of shifts at the poultry-gutting plant in Lowell where they all worked.

"This'll be paved in no time," the realtor had said, looking at our curve in the road, rocking back and forth, sucking on something leftover in his teeth from lunch. "You got yourself a real deal here. Everything is shifting."

Our view to the right was open fields and distant construction of gigantic homes in a subdivision, The Vineyard. There, the stones on the homes were imported, rounded and gray, like something in New England. To the left, a potpourri of crankheads, Butterball and family's old river stone house, slumped on one side as if burdened, and past it the Guatemalan village's single crusty trailer and a dried-out hillside striped with silver commercial chicken houses. I'd dreamt of living out somewhere far away from the chicken farms I'd grown up around.

"All that'll be coming down soon," the realtor had said. He had waved his hand at what was disagreeable, including the stone house.

Butterball's mother hadn't invited me inside the two times I'd gone over. Each time, I had stepped around a hole in the porch, something growling, menacing and low beneath my feet. The first visit was to introduce myself and bring a chess pie, my grandmother's recipe, and the second to ask her to tell her youngest boy to quit slinging gravel at our roof. I'd never seen him do it, but I noticed a small chip or two in a window I blamed on him. Both times she kept the door tight to her shoulder and responded roughly the same to the greeting as the complaint. "Huh," she said. "Yeah, okay." I never got the pie plate back, and didn't want to ask for it either. Anticipating this, I had used a shitty one that had a big chip in it. Sometimes I wished the sinking pile of rocks would burn to the ground to improve our view, and the family with it. I don't have an endless supply of Christian charity and goodwill like my mother.

Turkey buzzards circled in the sky, spiraling down lazily into something rotten, probably improperly discarded carcasses cleaned off of commercial henhouse floors, waiting to be burned or turned into the litter dumps. The August heat was cranking up, the scent of chicken manure shifting with the warming breeze off fertilized fields. Inside our French Country Model #809 home (inspired by the elegant but simple lifestyle of Provence, it had said on the plans), I could hear shrill whistles and crashing, wonky noises of morning cartoons. John banged on something in the garage. I brushed the remaining scales from my fingers and walked around to the opening.

"Coons ate the fish," I said. My voice lifted and cracked the way our daughter's did when she announced a new disappointment in life.

John, bent over a riding lawnmower, looked up from under his armpit. "What?" he said, like I had asked him what he wanted on a sandwich rather than announced a tragedy.

"They just took 'em," I said. I felt the heat of a tear slide from one eye, then another, and was immediately ashamed. John stood up, his hand cradling a socket wrench, and looked at me. He politely ignored my weeping over missing fish—he taught middle school biology and was accustomed to random outbursts of emotion.

"You sure?" he asked.

"Yes, I'm fucking sure!" I said, wiping my face. I hated it when he questioned me, like I had gone stupid since I became a stay-at-home mom. I had a graphic design degree from a softball scholarship at Arkansas Tech I was going to put to real use as soon as our daughter started kindergarten. "I know their ways."

"Their ways?" he said, and laughed. He pulled a piece of material from his back pocket and twisted the oily wrench in it. I saw it was one of the fancy napkins my aunt had given us for our wedding. She said it came from India. I kept these in my grandmother's antique buffet and used them only twice a year, at Thanksgiving and Christmas dinner. John looked down at the napkin in his hand and shoved it back in his pocket. I got gut-sick and sadder right there, felt the hate building in my neck where it liked to live, and turned and went into the kitchen.

Our kitchen was designed "family friendly" with a mud/laundry room off the garage and an open bar looking out into the living room that made me feel like a fry cook. It seemed like a good plan originally, but now I saw it was designed to trap me in one area for labor. Alexis, seeing me in the work zone, yelled that she wanted more Cocoa Puffs. "Now!" she said. Being a mother wasn't as fulfilling as advertised, not that I didn't experience a raw ache in my guts when she genuinely hurt herself or was feverish, or melt at her sudden affections. Not that I wouldn't defend her to the death from a rabid, koi-thieving coon attack. But whenever I was bored and numb from demands, her tears just another task to be addressed, I experienced a flagging doubt that I was contributing anything all that much by being there all the time. I looked at the side of her ponytailed head, her eyes glowing from reflected TV, mouth slack, and tried to remember the last time she was sweet.

John came into the kitchen, gave me a peck on the head, and grabbed his keys. "We'll get more, bigger ones, and they'll eat the coons if they come back. I gotta go pick up some things in town." Sometimes I had a hard time figuring if he possessed boundless optimism, or he simply didn't give a shit. Either way I could admire it, and I felt the tension in my neck lessen slightly. Alexis ran to him and whined that she wanted to go too, but John did a little dance, whirled her around, blew fart noises into her tubby belly, and said, "Not today, punkin'." He was an expert at waltzing in, both denying and delighting Alexis at the same time, with no ill consequences. After he left she lightly kicked the back door before turning her dissatisfaction back to me.

"Cocoa Puffs!" she said. She put her hands on her hips and made the pouty face her grandparents encouraged and photographed. We didn't live far from where me and John had grown up in Huntsville, so our parents had full access to their five-year-old granddaughter. They claimed we continued some kind of family legacy by building in that same narrow stretch of valley. Ancestors had banded together in one section of hills and fought off whatever discomfort and outlaws to build a life that lasted generations. I wondered what beauty they had imagined here, versus what they found. At times this gave us comfort. Other times we felt like failures for not making it outside the valley. My parents had a photograph of Alexis on the mantel amongst the stern great-great-grandparents who had named each bluff, each hollow surrounding us. They wore overalls and severe black dresses as if they were ready to work in the fields or be buried. In her photo, Alexis wore a pink tutu and T-shirt that said *Princess* (something they had never encouraged me to be), in that exact pose she now struck before me. I hated that fucking picture.

"You already had your breakfast," I said. And then listened to the many reasons why the first breakfast was insufficient and more sugar was necessary to survive. "Nope," I said. "Not open for discussion. Why don't you go outside and play?"

Alexis made indistinct noises, words stretched into whine, and stomped back into the living room for more cartoons. We'd purchased a slide, tire swing, monkey climber combo jungle gym and put small, rounded landscaping pebbles beneath it. "What are them fucking rocks for?" my father had asked. "For safety," I said. "From what?" he said. Wasps built nests in the tire swing that I was obliged to hose out every week in case Alexis learned to appreciate it, and the crossbeams gave the crows a place to perch and pick at the cornbread I threw out for songbirds. Next door I heard the rumblings of Butterball's rusty Z28, a car that didn't look like it had the capacity for movement, the catalytic converter removed for added annoyance. He slung a spray of gravel with his dramatic exit.

Within ten minutes after Butterball's departure the littlest one from next door was on the porch, pretending to look at my decorative ferns. Sometimes when his brother abandoned him, the boy showed up. I didn't encourage it. His mother was none too friendly the few times she had come over to get him, smoking and tapping her foot, scratching herself and ashing on my porch like I had inconvenienced her instead of the other way around. I don't know why people act like if you have one kid it's okay to dump strange ones on you like stray kittens. All kittens are cute. Not all kids are. When his older brother would fetch him he'd linger too long, adjusting his crotch and making statements that merited no response: *You like fish* or *I seen you was planting flowers*. No one ever bothered to apologize for abandoning the child to my care without notice.

There was a faint scratching noise at the door. I opened it and stared down at the kid, who, rather than make eye contact, broke off a fern leaf and looked past me into the house like he had forgotten something in there. He was puffy, like his brother used to be, and barefoot.

"Where's your mama?" I asked.

He shrugged and stuck the edge of the fern leaf in his mouth.

"Come on in," I said. The kid walked into the house with

the halting uncertainty of a stray cat, but nosed his way straight for the kitchen. "Gimme that," I said. I took the sodden fern leaf away from him and threw it in the trash. He tiptoed along the countertop until he saw the Cocoa Puffs. "Want some?" I asked.

His head did a slight tilt forward and back, and then he stared at his dirty feet while I poured out a bowl. Alexis heard the sound of sugar nuggets hitting porcelain and came trotting into the kitchen. She drew back when she and the kid made eye contact and hid halfway behind the door jamb. I didn't care much for her going anywhere near that house or those boys, and had told her so many times.

"I want some too," she said.

They settled in with their bowls, far apart in separate corners of the den, and watched cartoon animals beating the shit out of each other again and again. Almost two hours later, after I guiltily looked at curtains online, and one altercation over the boy touching Alexis's coloring books on the coffee table, John came back toting bags from both Home Depot and Lowe's. He also had a bucket containing three koi, bigger than the last.

"Too big for coons to wrestle," he said. He spotted the kid in the living room and nodded toward him, raising his eyebrows.

"Yup," I said.

"We should call somebody," he said.

"Yes, but you'll be asking for trouble."

John stared at the kids in the living room, considering the balance between trouble and civic responsibility. He reached into a sack on the counter, tossed me a beer, and walked to the French doors opening onto our backyard where Lola streamed away. "Pissing in perpetuity," he said.

I didn't hear the mother return, but noted Butterball wasn't back when she rang my doorbell. She picked at a scab on the side of her head with her pinky. "He here?" she said, smoke sliding out of her tired face as if she was too weary to exhale. I opened the door wider where she could see the boy in the living room. He looked up from a coloring book, like he'd been caught, and started to scoot over toward us.

"He's too little to be left alone like he is," I said. "You need to see to it that there's someone looking out for him when you leave."

"You got a pretty room here," the mother said. "Like out of a magazine." She said this as if it were an accusation rather than a compliment. She poked her scratching pinky at a dark chocolate loveseat sitting by a front window, lined with striped pillows in varying pale blues. I'd gotten it at T.J. Maxx. It looked to be waiting for a lady to relax there and read poetry in the soft light, or gaze out at the passing chicken trucks and Guatemalans and contemplate the sanctity of her home. I'd never sat in it since I'd put it there.

"If his brother can't see to him then he needs good day care," I said.

The mother sighed and tapped ash onto my porch, then looked dully at her spent cigarette and flicked it into my azaleas. She craned her neck to see what was taking the kid so long. He was gathering the pictures I had forced Alexis to allow him to color in her *Sea Friends* book, a scribbled squid and great white shark, both in orange. "That's real good," I'd said in that bullshit way everyone praises children now. He had stopped coloring, wiggled slightly, and ducked his head, pleased but uncertain what the correct response to praise was. It made me feel shitty that I didn't mean it.

"Well, come on," she said to the boy, and lit another.

Neither of them looked at me as they turned from the porch; the boy dragged his feet as if afflicted. I watched them walk back to their askew house, her hand gripping the back of his neck, smoke trailing from behind her frizzy head. The dog barked at them, high-pitched and insistent, until the woman said something sharp and low to make it shut up. Butterball was now back and standing in the yard, gazing in the general direction of Lola, love-struck, scratching his dick. A small garbage fire burned at the edge of our borders, stinking of plastic and chemicals.

I stuck my head into the garage. John was back at his lawn-mower, but with a new pack of utility rags open beside him. "Call whoever you need to call," I said.

The gravel started hitting the top of the roof again later that afternoon. First a single plunk, followed by a rattling drop into my flower bed, something I could have mistaken as a pine cone. Then a buckshot rain shower. I ran outside to yell at the kid, a single stone still making its rattling way to the azaleas below, but there was no one there. The dog lay limp from the heat in a burrowed-out hole, halfway under the foundation of the house. John offered to go talk to them, but I figured him making a call Monday morning was enough.

By Wednesday the new fish were dead. I found their swelling bodies, iridescent gold and white, floating sideways under the indifferent gaze of Lola. On Monday, with the help of Alexis, we had named them after Disney princesses. The sharp scent of bleach was apparent. I called John at work, and he told me to just calm down until he got home.

"And then what?" I said. "After I'm all calm and you're here, then what?"

I called the sheriff's office and got the same tired woman I had spoken to before about the Guatemalans. "Honey, we'll try and send somebody out to look at it," she said. I went to the pond and turned Lola off. There was something about her pouring that didn't seem right while the bodies were still there, bobbing lightly, floating only for John to witness. I took photographs of the fish for evidence before burial, digging a big hole over near the neighbor's yard by their burn pile. The skinny Rottweiler about to strangle itself to get at me, barking hoarse. A darkness could be seen behind one of the windows. No one came outside. The dog twisted and strained against the chain, its barks no more than raspy air.

"Want one, shithead?" I said, real sweet and soft, and threw him Ariel first. The fish body, rigid, smelling of chemicals, landed with a thunk in front of the startled animal. The dog leaped back, withdrawing closer to the crumbling foundation of the house. "How about Belle then?" I said. "Sink your teeth into that." I could hear the muted sounds of Alexis calling for me, louder as she stepped out on the back patio. I reached for Cinderella's stiff body and paused to look at the delicate beauty of her scales up close. As the dog crept toward the two fish, gaining interest, the back screen door of the stone house flung open. The mother came tottering out, followed by Butterball and the kid.

"What are you doing?" she said.

Butterball didn't have his usual reflective shades on, and without concealment his eyes appeared small with dark circles, his face more childlike. He looked more like a scared, misshapen old boy than a misshapen young man. Little brother hovered behind older brother's sagging jeans. I held Cinderella and saw them standing there as uncertain as creatures disturbed under a rock and began to feel ashamed for all of us. The kid reached up to touch his brother's ass, at which the teenager snapped a hand back to slap him away, like he was waving away a fart. "Yeah," Butterball said. He stepped forward.

"Giving your dog old fish," I said. "But if you got a reason he shouldn't eat it . . ."

"Fuck you and your fish," the mother said. She kicked at either Ariel or Belle and knocked off her flip-flop. "Keep your goddamned fish to yourself and mind your own fucking business."

Alexis called for me again. I turned around to see her edging closer. She was wearing the pink tutu outfit her grandparents had given her. I hadn't yet told her the princesses were all dead. I chucked Cinderella in the hole and turned away.

"Stay away from my house," I said. I picked Alexis up and held her to me, walking quickly toward our home. I didn't look back at the neighbors, but heard muttered curses and the thump of what turned out to be Ariel, or maybe Belle, falling close behind us. Alexis didn't ask about the fish, as if fish-throwing was a given around here. She put a knuckle up to her mouth and gnawed lightly on it, like she used to when she was a baby, squinting back over my shoulder with an expression I didn't quite recognize, neither fearful nor sad, as if thoughtfully plotting some dark revenge. "How about some Cocoa Puffs?" I said.

John lectured me briefly about engaging with the enemy when he got home. "Stay the fuck away from them. Especially when I'm not here. What if they had done something more than throw a fish?"

"They did do something more!" I said. "They killed them, to start with."

"Guess they heard from child services."

Alexis liked to draw wiggly figures she called fish princesses. One blobby, gold and pink creation she gave to John to hang on the refrigerator. The Fish Princess was wearing a tutu.

"Jesus Christ," I said, and tore it down before dinner.

A policeman came to take a dead fish report the next morning. When I saw the squad car in the drive, I felt a momentary chill inside, the way I always feel around cops. Like I should run up into the woods and hide further in the hills even if I haven't done anything wrong. The biggest sons of bitches I ever knew from high school had become policemen. Bastards with badges. He had a country-cop saunter, a walk that said he could give a shit, was even vaguely amused, as he came up to the front door. I led him through the house to the backyard. He smiled and winked at Alexis, who stared back at him, unmoved.

"You say it was bleach?" he asked. "Can't really smell it." The officer stood a ways back to admire the fish pond. "Nice water feature."

"And then when I was trying to bury the fish, they threw one at me," I said.

"Who did?"

"The ones that did this," I said. "Over there." We walked to the edge of the yard and stood beside the freshly dug earth.

"You saw them poison the fish," he said, "and then they come over and grabbed them up?"

"Well, no, but I know it was them. Their dog wouldn't shut up so I threw one at it."

"You did?" He seemed to find this funny. "I'll need to have a word with them. Thank you, ma'am."

While the cop went next door I surveyed my yard: a struggling dogwood transplanted from my parent's farm, a dry bird bath, hand-painted mailbox, grass patchy with stray chicken feathers and dandelions, and the fish grave. I always thought I would wind up in town proper, away from the fields and scrub oak–lined fences, the burned-out remnants of trailers and chicken houses, away from people like our tweaker neighbors and cranked-up Guatemalans. I wanted a manicured, paved street with sidewalks. Real sidewalks.

Another truck of migrant laborers on their way to the chicken farms slowed down as it passed, a dry, fine dust billowing behind it. The men inside craned their necks to look at me and the squad car, and I heard the faint sound of tinny music from their radio. I stared back at the driver, who pulled in an arm that draped out the window and sped up. I watched them disappear around the curve. No one turned back around.

I went in the house and watched from the chocolate loveseat. The mother wasn't home, but Butterball stepped out on the porch and shut the door behind him. He pointed at our house a time or two. The policeman nodded, followed the line of his finger with his gaze, and nodded some more until he seemed satisfied.

"Ma'am," he said when he returned, "my best advice is to stay away from them, but this call is on record. Unfortunately, there's no way to prove anything."

"Fine," I replied, and shut the door.

I worked in the yard until John got home, Alexis beside me most of the time, to show the neighbors I wasn't going to take any more fish-killing kind of bullshit hiding out in the house. Alexis built things she called forts with sticks in the grass. "For fairy princesses," she said.

That night, in the early-morning hours, John and I were awakened by stones hailing onto the roof, followed by a spray of rocks at the windows. Looking into the semidarkness I saw the ember light of the mother's cigarette. She stooped to pick up another handful of gravel. She flung once more with a limp wrist. The sharp crack of the gravel hitting the window forced me to step back. Stones dribbled onto the roof. She stood there a second more, seeing us peering out from our home like treed raccoons before she flicked one last cigarette into our yard and turned to her car. The roar of Butterball's Z28 was heard sliding around on the dirt road as he drove away, and then the coughing start of the mother's engine.

"Maybe that was their last *fuck you*," John said. "I've got one back if it wasn't."

As the morning light grew stronger, so did the glow from within the stone house. Whatever shit they hadn't taken with them absorbed the smoke, the heat, perhaps embraced its welcome release. A cleansing.

"Told you they were cooking," John said, and picked up the phone to call the fire department.

"No," I said. "Wait."

We watched the gathering flames work upon the rotten insides of the house until the first flickers emerged, exploring the fresh air outside.

"Go ahead," I said.

After John called, we saw that Alexis was sleeping through everything and went out to watch the house swollen with fire. We stood back from the growing flames, hearing small explosions and pops from within, who knows what remnants of poison released in the heat. An electrical wire flipped and sparked near the collapsing porch. Two truckloads of Guatemalans on their way to work pulled over to watch. We spoke to one another in different tongues but seemed to convey the same message as we pointed and nodded. The Guatemalans looked infinitely weary. I turned back to see our own house in its soft, orange light. The colors I'd chosen for the exterior, Lambskin and Froth, looked beautiful in the warm light of the burning house, like a sculpted cake, except for a notable absence in the backyard. Lola was gone, riding the open highway in a rusted-out Z28 with Butterball wide, wide awake, probably stroking her naked tit.

A gathering of old men from the volunteer fire department hung around drinking coffee until midmorning. Happy. House fires weren't common; you were always lucky to be rousted from your retirement to attend one. And this one was better off to let burn. Toxic. The same officer who took the dead fish report was there, but this time he took notes and seemed to find me less funny. "You'd better stay away from what's left of this mess until we can get it cleaned up," he said. We all stood with our hands on our hips, shaking our heads. John promised to bring back motion detection lights to put on the house after work, but I didn't think they would be back, as the officer agreed. "Probably running to their next rat hole," he said. By noon, everyone was gone.

Midafternoon and another truck rattles past, full of birds and slinging feathers and trailing the smell of shit and fear. Bodies are tucked into dirty white balls, giving up whatever hope can flicker in a chicken's little brain. Others, stunned, dead-eye the passing landscape, more colors, shapes, and sounds than they have ever seen inside a commercial poultry house. Trucks carting chicken-catchers follow. Brown faces, empty with exhaustion, see me standing by the azaleas, surrounded by decorative lawn ornaments, holding a fistful of dandelion roots, a little girl in a pink tutu sitting in the grass beside me playing with brightly colored ponies. I wonder if any of them are our Guatemalans from nearby. I stop and stand to watch them pass and then peer back at my house. I imagine how I would crop this scene. With the afternoon haze of airborne dust giving the sky a golden glow, the dry, yellow fields surrounding us look almost like something from a magazine. The woods beyond conceal the limestone bedrock that my ancestors struggled to scratch a living from. Our French Country #809, flowers and garden, looked a fruitful place, safe from invasion. A peaceful image of a distant land where generations upon generations drink wine and watch their children grow. If you looked at it just right, it could be something beautiful.

Noah Kalina

TAO LIN is the author of six books of fiction and poetry, including *Richard Yates*, his second novel, which was published in 2010.

# 51 hours
## by tao lin

ack woke ~2:30 p.m. and talked to Daniel on Gmail chat. Daniel said he and Allie didn't sleep last night and were getting drugs then eating brunch to celebrate Allie getting fired from the waitressing job she got a few days ago. Jack showered and left his apartment and text-messaged Daniel that his Adderall shipment, which arrived once a month from a college professor, hadn't arrived. Daniel said he didn't know if he could stay awake for a party that night without Adderall and asked if Jack wanted to buy Adderall from his drug dealer. Jack said he would contribute twenty dollars for the 11-for-$110 deal. Daniel didn't respond. Jack went to a café and drank a large iced coffee and created what he viewed as "oxy water" by dissolving a small plastic bag of blue-yellow paste consisting of OxyContin, a little Klonopin, and a little Adderall in a Tea's Tea bottle of water. He'd made the paste, accidentally, by washing his jeans in the bathtub with those drugs in the pocket. He text-messaged Daniel that he felt like most of the OxyContin disappeared, or something, when it turned into a paste, because it didn't seem like the same amount as before it became a paste. Daniel responded with a panicked-seeming text message of two compound sentences speculating on what happened to the OxyContin. Jack grinned and responded for Daniel to stay calm and that the OxyContin was safe, in a Tea's Tea bottle. Jack went online at the library feeling a little high from the Klonopin-Adderall paste on the outside of the OxyContin packet he'd licked clean, combined with the iced coffee and an amount of OxyContin he'd licked from his fingers. A few hours later he met Frank and Daniel on the second floor of a building on the Lower East Side for the one-year anniversary of an Internet company. Jack drank half the bottle of oxy water. Daniel drank the other half. It was ~9:30 p.m. "Should we go to the other thing now?" said Frank about a gallery in Brooklyn that was showing Jack's art tonight in a group show.

"Are you okay, man?" said Frank on the train to Brooklyn.

"Yes," said Jack and focused on not moving or thinking.

"You don't look okay," said Frank while grinning at Daniel.

The train arrived and they walked five blocks to the art gallery, which was someone's apartment. Jack looked at his art on a wall. He went in the bathroom, then with Frank and Daniel to the roof. "I feel a lot better," he said and went downstairs and said hi to Laila who was holding a glass of wine and seemed sober and who introduced Jack to two people whose names he didn't try to remember. One said something nice about Jack's art and Jack made a noise while not looking at anything. Sara walked toward Jack who said, "This is Sara" and "This is Laila," and, as Sara was complimenting Laila's necklace, walked away, through a door, into a small room, and sat on a foam floor. Sara entered and sat by Jack and said Laila had said, "So, what's new?" to her, and that was when she knew it was time to walk away. Jack went to the roof and looked at Daniel and Frank seated next to each other grinning. "Jack," said Daniel. "Come here." Jack stood in front of Daniel and Frank a few seconds, then went downstairs and stood near Andrew who was talking to David about if a horse could win "best athlete of the year." Jack was aware of Laila in the distance talking to people. He went to the roof and stood by Justin and said, "Look at that kitchen," and pointed at a lower floor on another building. Justin said, "What kitchen?" and Jack moved close to the edge and almost fell off the roof. He asked if

Justin would have felt responsible if he had died. He went downstairs and said, "Hey, I'm leaving, just wanted to say bye," to Laila, who was sitting on the floor, and they hugged. Laila seemed incoherent and unable to stand.

Jack stood by Daniel and Andrew in the hallway.

"I used Adderall for the first time the other day," said Andrew.

"Oh, sweet," said Jack. "Did you like it?"

"Yeah. I didn't think it would work."

"How many milligrams did you use?"

"Forty," said Andrew.

"Jesus," said Jack.

"I used twenty and it wasn't working so I used another twenty."

"Nice," said Jack.

Laila was walking toward them holding an unlit cigarette dangling between two fingers, barely maneuvering the hallway. "I already said bye to her," said Jack to Daniel. "I already said bye to her," he said to Andrew.

"I thought you were leaving," she said.

"Bye," said Jack. "I am."

A few minutes later she was moving toward him from the other direction. She moved her head toward his head and said, "I'm on 'shrooms," with unfocused eyes, and moved past him in the hallway, in the opposite direction of the exit.

About ten minutes later Daniel, Frank, Andrew, Jack got in a taxicab to Manhattan Inn. Jack ordered ribs. Daniel and Frank ordered an appetizer of chicken wings to share. Andrew said, "Why doesn't she stop dancing?" Jack looked at a woman dancing alone. Daniel and Frank ignored Andrew, whose eyes, in response, seemed to unfocus a little before refocusing elsewhere. Jack thought about saying something. He picked up his glass

and drank water. Frank left to sleep. Daniel left the table to talk
to other people who had come from the gallery. It was ~1:45 a.m.
Andrew said he was "good friends" with his roommate, an Asian
girl with an administration job in a nightclub, then left to sleep.
Jack ate ribs alone at the table. "I thought you were a vegetarian,"
someone said to him after a few minutes.

"No, I'm eating ribs," said Jack.

"I thought you didn't eat meat," said the person.

"I eat meat," said Jack.

"Oh, I didn't hear you," said the person. "I thought you said
you weren't eating meat. But you're eating ribs."

Daniel returned to the table holding a drink. "You should
grow an enormous afro, without any warning, for your next author photo," he said.

Jack, an artist and a writer, laughed and paid for his food and
left to sleep.

He woke ~2:30 p.m., ate three mangoes, looked at the Internet,
text-messaged Daniel, slept from ~3:30 p.m. to ~8:30 p.m., e-
mailed Frank he was staying in tonight. He exercised in his room
and showered. His Adderall had arrived and was in the kitchen
and he moved it into his room. He went to a café and drank a
large iced coffee with no ice and went to the library and worked
on things until ~12:30 a.m. He bought bananas, a mango, a cucumber, and walked toward his apartment. He saw a text message from Daniel that said, *come hang out, Frank bought a bunch
of speed*, and walked a few blocks to a bar and into the bathroom—which had a second door, leading outside—and splashed
water to his face, dried off, went through the second door to the
bar's outdoor area where Daniel, Frank, Maggie were standing
talking. Jack and Daniel began arguing about something while
grinning. Jack said Daniel needed to "lay off the eggplant," ref-

erencing a joke they had about how Daniel had been eating egg-plant as a drug and was now heavily dependent on it. Frank said his eyes were red because of cat allergies.

Daniel, Frank, Maggie, Jack stood on the sidewalk outside the bar discussing where to go to snort Frank's crystal meth. They crossed the street to Harry's apartment, went upstairs, stood in a large dark room of sofas, a TV, an open kitchen, a corner table with two computers. Dance music was playing loudly. Harry was hugging people from behind, or from the sides, while making loud noises.

"Harry seems out of control," said Jack.

"He hasn't done speed before," said Frank.

Jack peeled his mango alone in darkness at the kitchen sink and ate it, then walked elsewhere and noticed Daniel, Frank, Maggie in a bathroom with the door not fully closed. Jack pushed at the door. "It's me," he said and went inside. Maggie was sitting on the bathtub's edge. Daniel and Frank were sitting on the floor, around the toilet. "We thought you left," said Daniel.

"I wouldn't just leave," said Jack.

"It seems like you, of all people, would just leave," said Daniel, putting crystal meth on the toilet cover and crushing it with his debit card. Frank asked if Jack wanted some and Jack said, "Yes, if that's okay." Frank sneezed a little while moving his rolled-up twenty-dollar bill toward the crystal meth.

"Jesus," said Daniel. "Be careful."

"Why are you berating him?" said Jack. "It's his drugs."

"Bro," said Daniel and grinned at Jack a little.

"It's his," said Jack. "And he's sharing it with us."

They each snorted a line of crystal meth, then stood in the main room where ~fifteen people seemed to be hugging each other repeatedly while talking loudly.

"What is this?" said Jack.

"A rich person's apartment," said Daniel.

"Sweet," said Jack.

About ten minutes later Daniel, Frank, Maggie, Jack went to Legion, a bar a few blocks from Harry's apartment. Maggie went to the bathroom. Jack sat on a padded seat.

"Seems bleak," he said after a few seconds.

"What's wrong with you tonight?" asked Frank.

"There aren't any girls here for me," said Jack.

"Let's dance," said Daniel.

"I'm depressed," said Jack.

Frank and Daniel walked away. Jack looked at his phone. He stared at an area of torsos. He walked outside. He text-messaged Daniel that he was going to Khim's to *stock up on eggplant*.

In Khim's he felt energetic and calm, listening to Rilo Kiley through earphones, and put an organic beef patty, two kombuchas, organic bananas, alfalfa sprouts, arugula, some other things in his basket and paid. Walking toward Legion, Jack saw Harry approaching from the opposite direction with a troubled facial expression and sweat on his forehead and other areas of his face. Harry passed without looking at Jack. At Legion, Frank and Daniel were outside, vaguely arguing about something. Daniel went inside. Jack walked toward Frank who said he and Daniel were doing a line in the back room when a security guard came toward them and he threw the bag of crystal meth somewhere and Daniel was now inside looking for it.

"Where's Maggie?" asked Jack.

"In White Castle," said Frank.

They crossed the street to White Castle and sat with Maggie in a booth. Jack put his groceries on the table. "Chicken rings," he said about a poster on a wall. "To make chicken rings they would need to, like, mold the meat into rings, right?"

"I'm worried about Daniel," said Frank.

"He'll be in jail for, like, ten years if he gets caught," said Jack. "He said he has a warrant for his arrest in Colorado."

"Jesus," said Frank.

"It's better if Daniel goes to jail than you," said Jack. "He's in debt to like five people and needs like six hundred dollars in one week, for rent, and is unemployed and owes me seventy dollars. Whereas you have a real job and a nice apartment."

Maggie went to the bathroom.

"If Daniel goes to jail I'll remove his debt to me, I think," said Jack. "We could make a blog about him and mail him letters."

"A blog," said Frank, seeming worried. "Jesus."

"Should we go look for him? I'll go look for him," said Jack and crossed the street to Legion and walked to the back room and read a text message from Daniel that said, *come outside*. On the sidewalk Daniel, walking away from Legion ahead of Jack, said Frank had panicked and threw the bag of crystal meth under a table. "He shouldn't have done that," said Daniel. "He panicked, like a little bitch."

"He has a high-paying job," said Jack.

"Shouldn't I get some of this speed, since I was put in a position where I could've gotten in trouble?"

"If you want," said Jack. "Seems like, yeah, if you want."

Daniel stared ahead with a distracted facial expression.

"Frank and Maggie are in White Castle," said Jack. "My groceries are in White Castle. Where are we going?"

"Let's go to your room to do some of this speed," said Daniel.

They were on a street with no people or moving cars.

"It's too far," said Jack. "Just snort it off your hand."

Daniel removed a rock of crystal meth from the bag and put

both his hands in his jeans pockets. Jack said, "What are you doing, isn't it just going to, like, fall through your pants?" and ripped a page from his Moleskine journal and said Daniel could use it to contain the meth. Daniel was distractedly looking in different directions.

"You should snort it off the Lincoln," said Jack.

"There isn't a Lincoln here," said Daniel.

"That seems like a Lincoln," said Jack pointing at a car.

"That's a Pontiac," said Daniel.

"You should hide between two cars to do it," said Jack.

Daniel walked between two cars and kneeled, facing away from Jack, who photographed Daniel with his cell phone and sent the photograph to his own Gmail account and to Daniel's cell phone.

"Good job," said Jack walking toward White Castle.

"You know I don't do this to friends, usually," said Daniel, looking into the distance.

"You just did it," said Jack grinning. "I mean, what do you mean?"

"I mean, do you think it's okay I did that?"

"Seems fine," said Jack.

"I was put in a dangerous situation."

"Seems fine," said Jack.


"You threw the bag onto this little shelf," said Daniel to Frank in White Castle. "I was looking on the ground for it. The bag was open so I don't know how much fell out."

In Jack's room Daniel, Frank, Jack—Maggie had left to sleep—each snorted a line of crystal meth. Daniel looked at Jack's collection of time-release Adderall and questioned Jack about why one capsule was open. Jack said it broke open in the envelope. Daniel repeatedly questioned Jack about how much of the capsule was missing, implying that the person who mailed Jack the Adderall had removed some from each capsule. Jack spoke for ~ten minutes about having been tricked, saying things like, "I'm going to message her right now telling her I know one of these capsules only has twenty milligrams and that I want an explanation, right now," in a sarcastically outraged voice while signing into Facebook and typing the message to the person, asking Daniel if he should try to get the three books he had traded to the person, who was separate from his monthly shipment person, returned to him. At some point Jack felt unable to discern if Daniel knew he was being sarcastic, which caused Jack to increase his sarcasm, until he felt that he was saying things only to entertain himself. Daniel and Frank went into Jack's roommate's room and Jack heard the word "Fuckbuttons" and went to his roommate's room and said he had talked about Fuckbuttons last night. Daniel said Jack hadn't. Daniel said he and Frank had but Jack hadn't. "Are you sure?" said Jack.

"Where were we last night?" said Daniel.

"At . . . some . . . thing," said Jack after a few seconds.

"Is Shawn Olive your boyfriend?" said Frank to Jack's roommate.

"No," she said. "We're good friends."

Daniel, Frank, Jack went into Jack's room. There was some tense discussion about a book by Jack's friend Brandon that Jack published a year ago. Daniel seemed to be saying that the book was boring and that he didn't know why Jack published it. Daniel and Frank left and Jack cooked 70 percent of his organic beef patty and ate it with flax seeds, arugula, alfalfa sprouts, cucumber, tamari, lemon juice, olive oil. It was ~4:30 a.m. Jack ingested ~fifteen milligrams of Adderall and worked on things on his MacBook, laying stomach-down on his bed, sometimes e-mailing Daniel who was at his apartment a few blocks away and was responding within a few minutes to each e-mail. They decided not to sleep and to meet at 10 a.m. to go to the Museum of Modern Art. It was ~6:45 a.m. For the next few hours Jack sometimes stood and ingested a few milligrams of Adderall, each time noticing that the sunlight through his two large windows seemed gray. He e-mailed Daniel ~9:50 a.m. that he was naked on his bed and hadn't showered. Daniel responded that he was also naked and hadn't showered. About an hour later Jack e-mailed Daniel, *where the fuck are you*, and Daniel responded, within a minute, that he was still naked on his bed.

About thirty minutes later they met, got on the train, got off at Bedford Avenue. They walked to Rockin' Raw which wasn't open yet. It was raining a little. One of them said something about how the Museum of Modern Art would probably be extremely crowded because it was Sunday and within a few seconds both agreed that they shouldn't go there. They talked about going to LifeThyme and the garden. Jack asked if Daniel wanted to go to the bookstore. Daniel said, "Not really," but that he would go if Jack wanted. They decided to sit in a café called Verb to decide what to do next. They walked there and sat and each ingested ten milligrams of Adderall. Daniel removed a glass jar with a peanut butter label on it from his backpack and poured ~four ounces of whiskey into his iced coffee with a neutral facial expression. Jack asked what Daniel was going to do about his financial situation. Daniel said Frank had mentioned, a few days ago, hiring him to write promotional copy for Frank's band, but then didn't mention it again. Jack said he would help Daniel steal things today to sell on eBay or to thrift stores. They went in the bookstore and Daniel picked up the book that had almost exactly the same cover as Shawn Olive's book and showed it to Jack and said, "Shawn Olive." Jack said they had showed the book to each other a few nights ago and also talked about it for an amount of time. "I don't remember," said Daniel.

"It was in this store," said Jack. "Like two days ago."

They went outside and Jack pointed at an area of sidewalk and talked about how he and his ex-girlfriend had sold books sitting there. "We could do that," he said. "Let's do that, maybe." They walked aimlessly a few minutes. They walked toward Jack's apartment to get books to sell. A girl saw Daniel and stopped on her bike and said she was putting up fliers for an art fair on Berry Street and biked away. Daniel said he'd had sex with her and didn't know her name currently. Jack said her name was probably Kiki. They walked on Berry Street ~ten minutes and didn't see an art fair. They walked to East River Park. It was ~11:45 a.m. and cloudy. They decided it was time to snort the crystal meth Daniel stole from Frank last night. They walked to a somewhat isolated area of logs and cement blocks and sat and decided it would be better to snort the meth in Jack's room. They walked to Rockin' Raw and sat in the outdoor area. There were many large flies for some reason on the tables. They moved inside and Daniel went to the bathroom. Jack ordered a raw almond shake to go. They walked toward his apartment, ~fifteen blocks away, and Jack asked if Daniel snorted crystal meth in the bathroom. Daniel said he wouldn't do that without Jack and they went in a pizza place. Daniel walked toward Jack and said his debit card was either maxed out or not working from cutting so much speed.

Daniel stood in the middle of Jack's room and quietly said things about feeling "fucked" about his financial situation and also "generally." He kneeled to a table and created two lines of crystal meth. Jack asked what music Daniel wanted. Daniel didn't say anything. Jack put on "Heartbeats" by The Knife and they both laughed a little. Jack put on "Last Nite" by The Strokes and stopped it and said it was too depressing. Jack put on "Such Great Heights" by The Postal Service and stopped it and said, "What are we going to listen to?" and Daniel said to put "Such

Great Heights" back on, then snorted half his line and motioned for Jack to snort his. Jack moved some of his line into Daniel's half-snorted line, saying he only wanted five dollars worth and that it would be removed from Daniel's tab. "Seems like it's going to be impossible for me not to sneeze or something," said Jack and felt some difficulty in discerning "exhale" vs. "inhale" as he moved a rolled-up page of Shawn Olive's poetry collection in his right nostril toward the crystal meth by leaning his body off the bed. He snorted some then exhaled a little and some crystal meth spilled out on the table. Jack felt calm and amused as Daniel lightly berated him. "Frank did it a lot more," said Jack. "He, like, sneezed, or something. Seems like we're improving, if you view Frank and me as one person." He quickly snorted the rest of the crystal meth, then continued snorting areas of the table, including a small spot of what seemed to be colorful dust. "Stop," said Daniel and snorted the rest of his line. Jack lay on his bed in a splayed-out manner. Daniel continued to say that he felt depressed, but in a calmer voice. Jack stood and said they should go sell books now and put books, pens, blue spray paint, pieces of paper, some other things in his backpack and rolled up a small carpet. Daniel said they would probably sell three books and should probably just go to the garden instead, to relax. "Let's just try to sell books," said Jack. "If it doesn't work we can leave or just sit there relaxing. I'll give you all the profits."

They walked ~fifteen blocks and unrolled the carpet on the sidewalk. Jack put books on the carpet and wrote prices on paper and they sat with their backs against a wall. A British man picked up a book, looked at it a few seconds, said "I'll take it," gave Jack two dollars while looking in his wallet for a five-dollar bill. Daniel sincerely praised Jack's writing to the British man for a few minutes. The British man thanked them and walked away. Daniel said the British man had said "getting in on" in a hesitating manner, like he wasn't sure if he was getting the idiom right, and that Daniel had looked at Jack when he said that. Jack said he didn't notice. "He only gave me two dollars," he said. "Seems like a scam." An overweight, fashionable, shy-seeming girl bought two books without removing her large headphones or speaking. Four black male teenagers appeared. One, who seemed much more interested than the others, asked if he could read some of a book and then read some of it and laughed and said, "I'll take it."

"Sweet," said Jack.

"Do you like Adderall?" said Daniel.

"What is it?" said the teenager.

Daniel described it in a few sentences.

"So, it's like Ecstasy?" asked the teenager.

"Sort of," said Daniel. "Without the euphoria."

"Are you in?" said the teenager.

"No," said his friend. "But I'll watch you do it."

The teenager bought two Adderall.

Nick McDonnell appeared on a bike and introduced himself to Jack and said they had met before. Jack said, "I remember," and said something about KGB Bar. Nick McDonnell bought two books and said he looked forward to reading them. Jack asked him about his McSweeney's book. Jack said, "You know Mike Tonas, right?"

Nick McDonnell said he wished Mike would return from Portland.

"He's there permanently?" asked Jack.

"I think so," said Nick McDonnell.

Jack said he would move to Portland.

Daniel said, "You would?"

Jack said, "I don't know."

Nick McDonnell said he had a reading at The Half-King the next night, then rode his bike diagonally across Bedford Avenue.

"Do you know that person?" asked Jack.

"No," said Daniel. "Who is that bro?"

"He's rich," said Jack. "I liked his first novel. It was published when he was seventeen, I think. His father was the editor of *Rolling Stone* or something. His novel was blurbed by Hunter S. Thompson, Bret Easton Ellis, and Joan Didion and was just made into a movie by Joel Schumacher or someone. In the book the main character is a white person in high school who sells drugs. We should go to his reading. Tomorrow night."

They sat without talking ~twenty minutes.

"Should I use more Adderall," asked Jack.

"You're better to be around when you're on Adderall," said Daniel.

"What do you mean?" said Jack.

"You're really quiet without Adderall."

Jack went to Verb and ingested ten milligrams of Adderall, stood in line for the bathroom, peed, washed his face. He ran to where he and Daniel were selling books. The sky was mostly gray. There was some orange, red, purple in the distance. It was ~5:30 p.m. An Asian girl with a cell phone to her right ear approached and slowed a little and passed. She reappeared a few minutes later without a cell phone and said she knew who Jack was, from her coworkers. Jack said something about Adderall. "Are you guys cops?" she asked. "Because I'm waiting here to buy pot from someone. But I'm not sure about him." Daniel asked whom and she showed Daniel the drug dealer's business card. She bought two books and went to an ATM and returned and paid for three Adderall. She asked if Daniel or Jack had a driver's license, to move her friend's car from Crown Heights to the Graham L train stop for money. They talked about that a few minutes without concluding anything and it was quiet a few seconds and she removed a magazine from her bag and said she was translating an article from Mandarin and asked if Jack was good at translating. Jack said he couldn't read Mandarin. Daniel asked where she was from and after a few minutes she began talking about her boyfriend who went to India after college, then returned to America and died, a few years ago. Jack heard her say something about how her boyfriend's funeral had become a party—that, for some reason Jack didn't hear, it had been the same as a party—except everyone was wearing black.

# PART IV
## medicine

**MEGAN ABBOTT** is the Edgar-winning author of the novels *The End of Everything, Bury Me Deep, Queenpin, The Song Is You,* and *Die a Little.* Her work has appeared in *Wall Street Noir, Phoenix Noir, Detroit Noir, Queens Noir, Between the Dark and the Daylight: And 27 More Best Crime & Mystery Stories of the Year, Storyglossia, Los Angeles Times Magazine,* and *The Believer.* She is also the author of a nonfiction book, *The Street Was Mine: White Masculinity in Hardboiled Fiction and Film Noir,* and the editor of *A Hell of a Woman,* an anthology of female crime fiction. She lives in Queens, New York.

# everything i want
## by megan abbott

*for Courtney Love*

**Y**ou destroyed them, didn't you, doc?" one of the government men said, his arms deep in the drawers of the doctor's battered old filing cabinets. "All your records."

They wouldn't believe him when he said there was nothing to destroy. That he'd never kept files on any of his patients. He didn't need to keep records, to document any of it. Hundreds of patients over fourteen years of practice conducted in the second-floor office of the old Reefy Building, so much care woven into its fraying rugs, so many tears sunk deep into the heart pine floors. He could tell you everything about any of them.

"At a certain point," he said, "I could just look at them and know."

He remembered a motion picture he saw once, years ago, when he still indulged in leisure on an errant Sunday. A man sees what life would be like if he had never existed, his town a ruin, his family shorn, the world transformed into a nest of teeming vice. We would all like to believe we matter so much, he thought. That we are holding back the dam. But in his case, he knew it to be true. All those lonely souls who had darkened his office doorstep, who waited for him in the morning and lurked under the hallway sconces at night, who telephoned him at all hours, their voices keening in his ear.

If he had never arrived in town, they would still be shadow-living, tucked behind drawing room drapes, hiding under their office desks, crying into pocket squares on the bus ride home.

Life is hard. The world is punishing. These are the things he knew. In the face of such fermenting loss, the inconstant racket that is the only respite from sinking despair, why shouldn't he give them some joy?

He would always remember it, that icy December morning when he first hammered the *C. Tremblay, MD* sign on his office front door. Balanced on the window sill, his transistor radio crackled with news of Albert Schweitzer receiving the Noble Peace Prize. A man in Oslo recounted a story about how young Albert, traveling on a river in Africa, experienced an Important Moment. Gazing on the rays of the sun shimmering on the water, the abundant beauty of tropical forest, wild beasts at rest on the river banks, it was as though an "iron door had yielded, the path in the thicket had become visible." Suddenly, a phrase came to him: *Ehrfurcht vor dem Leben*. Reverence for life.

*"It is the youth of today who will follow the path indicated by Albert Schweitzer,"* the radio man was saying as Dr. Tremblay brushed the sawdust from the door face. *"All through his long life he has been true to his own youth and he has shown us that a man's life and his dream can become one."*

The doctor stood back and observed his handiwork, the porcelain enamel sign gleaming. Until that moment, he had never once felt he belonged anywhere. From that day forward he devoted himself to all those who sought his care, working harder and harder as the years passed.

For the last four years he had seldom left those careworn 250 square feet.

Who knew, after all, when Mrs. Neel would need to be lifted from deepest summer sorrows by the sight of the incandescent bulb glowing in his window nigh on two a.m.? Who knew when Mr. Cass, once nearly three hundred pounds and could not pick up his toddling daughter off the floor, might ask for help to fight the sound of his long-dead mother's voice telling him to clean his plate, clean all the plates?

No, he needed to be there, and so he spent his nights nestled on his tucker-leathered davenport, wrapped in an afghan lovingly knitted by Mary Floss, the proprietress of the BRE-Z Laun-Der-Rite and a woman with more than her share of dooming sorrows: two sons lost in Brittany and Kursk and a bleary husband consumed by reckless habits far worse than her own, which the doctor didn't consider a habit but a salve, a balm, a protection from the glaring sight of her mottled hands. Days spent, hands in lye, packing bachelor bundles in stiff blue paper, and the only pleasure to be had was the time with her knees clenched tight between his own, the blooming syringe settling deep in her arm, and her eyes flickering to high heaven.

Oh, Mary Floss, you deserve that, and so much more.

He was born fifty-two years ago to a sad-faced woman with no husband and a physician father with a long dark coat for whom she made meals and played the piano every evening. Within an hour of his birth, his grandfather took him from his mother's weakened arms, removed him from the house, and delivered him to one of the hospital nurses, a woman whose own infant girl had died in the crib of inanition many months before. Her breasts were still full, which she understood as a strong portent. Taking the newborn to her grieving chest, she determined to raise him as her own.

In her fruit cellar, the nurse kept a steady store of liniments, balms, demulcents, vitae, physics, and medical and homemade compounds gathered from her workplace and conjured through her own ministrations. Such is the way he learned the secrets of the body, the mind, and the heart. As he grew older and showed the facility and, she said, a native kindness, she taught him to understand the mystical properties of medicines, the ways that chemistry and the natural world and modernistic technology can all work in harmony. And that medicine is at once art, science, and magic.

One day, the nurse took him by the hand into her dark bedroom and, touching her lower belly with a trembling hand, she said that of all the things she had taught him, this he must remember most: when you have something eating you from the inside, whether it be of mind, body, or spirit—because these things are one—then you truly and at last understand what pain means and how it must be stopped. For herself, she halted it—or held it at bay—by means of the milky glass of ergot and morphine that she kept on her bedside table. And she halted it more and more as her body grew smaller and her eyes sunken. When he was thirteen, the nurse died, her body found by him in the fruit cellar in a state of undress, her hand still curled around that milky glass. Her face was both ruined and serene.

From this point forward, he made his own way. His grandfather arranged, via his lawyer, to give him sufficient funds to continue his schooling in a private young men's academy 250 miles upriver. Eventually, he ended up at a small medical college, but these details were not important to him, even as they were happening. The only thing that he recalled from those years was that he worked very hard and lived as if almost in a dream. All that mattered was that one day he would have his own practice and meet the needs of all his patients as they sought meaning and value in their lives.

This mission came to him during his first Important Moment, which occurred when he spent three days with a young girl in Marfa, Texas, a girl with green ribbons twisted through long braids. He met her at a roller rink where she always held one leg aloft behind her. For seven years, she had worn a cast from the base of her neck to her knees and elbows, she told him, and now had one built-up shoe to accommodate the right leg shriveled still. When she skated, it was as if the cast had never been there at all, and her body was beautiful, weightless.

The last night, she took him out into a large field astride the Chinati Mountains. When dusk fell, mysterious orbs of light appeared on the horizon then rose in the sky dancing wild tangos with each other in great pulses of blue, yellow, and a kind of phosphorescent green. As he gazed in wonder, hand in hers tightly, knuckles burning, the girl told him these lights had saved her father during a terrible blizzard, lighting his way to the shelter of a cave.

Then, holding tight to his arm, the girl took off her long boot and showed him her withered leg, luminescent under the ghostly lights.

He touched her leg with trembling hands and she looked up at the sky and said, Do you know what these lights signify? And she asked it again and again until she started crying. Her face white from the gloomy lights, he at last knew beauty and magic and wanted to cure her and everyone else.

For seven years, he worked in the orthopedic ward at a hospital in Darke County, and then four years in the army. But it was not until hanging his sign on the door of the second-floor office of the Reefy Building that he felt his life had become his own. At last, he could minister to his patients in his way, in the intimate confines of that place, behind the beveled-glass door, seated on his examination table, their legs dangling, so vulnerable. And the comfort they felt the minute they looked into his eyes and saw only kindness, relief, release.

One, a jaundiced fellow with a pencil mustache, came to him weekly, nattily dressed and smelling of Violet Mints that nudged from the top of his smooth breast pocket. Before the doctor, he had been stricken by such dolor he could not rise from bed and thus had lost his job. Now, he ran the Imperial dining room at the country club and never, ever stopped smiling.

Another, why, before the doctor, he was in dire straits. Mr. Alfred Matheson. The owner of the sprawling emporium on Chess Street, but something had come undone after his beloved daughter moved to California to experience new things. Since then, Mr. Matheson had begun spending evenings at Watson's Bar, drinking and playing the same mournful Irish ballads over and over on the juke box and not letting anyone else put coins in. Long after the commuter trains had stopped rolling into the station across the street with late-returning men in rumpled suits and red Strouss' bags, he would sit under the fairy lights and speak to all who would listen, saying dark things about how the Atomic Age, like man himself, was born in suffering.

Privately, Dr. Tremblay could not disagree.

"Did you see him?" whispered the clerks at Mr. Matheson's store, the ones who spent their days dipping their dirty hands in the undergarments bins and strolling the bright aisles as if kings. "He is not sound." They would talk about how he laughed for no reason and sometimes cried into his desk blotter, shoulders heaving. And the way he licked his lips and moaned when Dinah Shore came on the radio, because, he said, Dinah hails from Winchester, Tennessee, and had polio as a child, as did his sister.

But they could not see what the doctor could. They lacked the glowing eye in the center of his forehead which no one could see but his patients. The one that said: All I need is to be tended to. That is all I need.

And the doctor did. For Albert Matheson, a steady supply of

blue pills, each one shaped lovingly like a heart, and twice-weekly injections customized for his particular and exceptional (they were all exceptional) circumstances. When needed, twice a day.

"You told them you were giving them rejuvenators, regulators, revivifiers," the government man said. "But what we found were various mixes of vitamins, enzymes, procaine hydrochloride, dextroamphetamine amobarbital, methamphetamine, and . . . human placenta."

"I gave them life," the doctor replied.

Without him, he knew what many would do. There was one young woman who, before the doctor arrived in town, had relied on the proprietor of an exotic notions store on Tamm Street to provide her with a hobo bindle filled with morphine-soaked raisins she could suck on all day. Another, a crater-faced young man, consumed by misery of a variety too dark to penetrate, would surely return to his prior acts of desperation, sneaking, in the blue-dark of night, to Acme Farms to steal amphetamines from the jobby throats of chickens, who produce eggs with sumptuous rapidity so dosed. Who but the doctor could look at this nervous young man and know all there was to know for what his inner being cried? Who knew what was needed to salve the wounds of a life spent feeling Other?

What would become of Eleanor Lang, a housewife with four children under five and a husband who spent six days a week traveling for Pan Am? Without the doctor's cross-marked wonders doled out in strict tidy rows she would surely have finally done the thing she threatened to do many times before. Twice, this tiny woman nigh on five feet tall had taken a hand drill and once a Bakelite phone handle and once more an awl pick and vowed to stop the train bearing down on the center of her skull. With the doctor gone, the only thing to stop Eleanor Lang would be the experimental surgery her husband kept reading about in *The Rotarian*. No better than the hand drill, the awl.

"Conspiracy to violate federal drug laws relating to stimulant drug. Willfully, knowingly, unlawfully selling, delivering, and disposing of a stimulant drug, namely 22.1 grams of amphetamine sulfate on the following dates—"

"I never sold them," Dr. Tremblay said. "I never sold anything."

"You didn't charge for your services?" the government man said snidely. "You're just the old charity ward, eh?"

"Young man, if you think I did this for pecuniary gain," the doctor replied, his eyes grave—so grave and portentous that even the government man straightened and drew down his propped leg from the desk—"then I deeply misunderstood you. It is rare, but it does occur. Because when I looked at you, past the brute ignorance of your generation and type, I thought I saw something else. Something deeper. Perhaps I was wrong."

Yes, at times even he could not forestall all horrors. A patient who comes only once leaves his office, returns home, and assaults his lady friend with a telephone. A young woman triples her prescribed dose and takes a meat fork to her roommate, then to herself. A knot-browed young man calls at all hours to tell the doctor his skin is radioactive, that his dead mother watches him through a periscope, that his father, long dead, has poisoned the city reservoir, and that we, all of us, are drinking toxins every day. Troubled souls who did not trust enough in him and whose damage is too ancient for him to undo. But are these aberrations to be laid at his creased-leather feet?

As much as he told himself otherwise, he did in fact know he couldn't cure every heart he held in his aging hands. He couldn't even rightly reckon with all the mysteries of the heart. The dark chambers invisible even to my physician's-eyed scalpel. But he had tried.

The one they called to testify—why, watching Mrs. Moses-Pittock nearly brought him to acrid tears. A very wealthy woman, age sixty-two, with the daintiest of ways, and a thick coil of gleaming pearls that looped five times around her neck like an Egyptian snake charmer. For three years she had been coming several times a week for shots, sliding her alligator wallet from her handbag, a handbag soft as curling caramel, and giving him bills crisp from the New Century Merchants Bank, which her father founded a hundred years ago. The newspapers said that he had injected her in the throat, as if she were a horse. Why would he do that? There was no need. It was a beautiful act, seated across from one another, his knees locked against hers, hers locked together.

She would speak to him only once the medicine was in the syringe. And then she was transformed, even before he pulled the plunger.

His grip on her stemlike elbow. The needle and its blooming rescue.

The blood floating like a pink balloon.

Then she would let her moon-shaped fingertips touch his lab coat, her eyelashes fluttering, the faint sound of her filigreed rings clicking against each other.

In court, she had made her grand way to the witness stand, Chez Ninon wool suit the color of a very bright olive, pilgrim pumps tapping the oak planks, and so seeming without trouble in all God's green world. But the doctor knew. He knew about her son's wayward life in Greenwich Village, and about her own private abuses to keep her body slim as the pea shoot her husband had married, abuses he had ceased. And he knew the thing that happened twenty years before, when she accepted that ride from her husband's business partner and the thing he did to her, her mouth pressed shut by his hand, in his gleaming roadster. He knew her suffering, and how to stop it.

After an hour or more of courtroom politenesses, of delicacy, and Mrs. Pittock's sweet-faced resistance, the prosecutor mopped his forehead with frustration. "Mrs. Pittock," the prosecutor said, "do you understand that these were narcotics? That he was putting your health at risk?"

"He has always been so kind," she said from the witness stand. "One August day, I was feeling so unwell I couldn't leave my bed. He walked the four miles to my home to deliver my medications. He has no car, you know. It was nearly 102 degrees. When I asked, *Aren't you warm?* he said, *Such luxuries I can't allow myself.*"

Listening in court, the doctor remembered walking under the barrel-arch ornamental plaster ceiling, tending to her in her damask-walled sitting room, her face white with woe. It was not a world the doctor knew. The doctor knew his aluminum percolator and the prickling static of his RCA.

"He made me feel like a princess," she said.

But it was not Mrs. Moses-Pittock with whom the government men were interested. The doctor knew this. The doctor knew that it had all begun with the scientist.

"I have a voice in me that speaks," the scientist told the doctor. "He says that I am a monster. He speaks to me late at night and at other times too. When I hear him, I cannot move. I cannot rise from bed. I cannot go to my office. I cannot perform my duties. I am no longer a man."

His name was Warren Tibbs of Tibbs Square, the tree-lined

common down on the central boulevard. He was a college physics professor, age forty-six but looked ten years older. He had four children, a wife with true yellow hair and a dimple in one corner, and a house that had been his father's and grandfather's, stately and American in all ways. All this, the sparkling sterling silver service and Hepplewhite chairs and a big brass front door that shone in the sun. But the sorrow in his eyes was five fathoms deep and Dr. Tremblay knew he must help him. His problem was not his heart condition, for which he took digitalis and quinidine daily.

For ten years, Warren confided to the doctor, he had been an important researcher at the Argonne National Laboratory just outside of Chicago, but the stresses of the job depleted him and he had retreated to his hometown. Warren told the doctor this while laying on the oriental carpet in his den, looking up at the doctor through hands laced across his eyes. The truth was, Warren added, his superiors felt his behavior had become erratic and his security clearances were rescinded. For which he was, he admitted, glad.

"Maybe," Warren said, his face in his hands now, "you have read of the Argonne Laboratory in the newspapers."

The doctor said he had.

"Did you know that radium used to be used to make a luminous paint?" he asked. "They used it for those clocks with the numerals that glow in the dark."

The doctor did indeed know this. Had read about it in the medical journals. He knew that the girls who worked in those clock factories painting those radium dials had all died of bone and brain cancer. It was their dentists who had discovered it.

"Every day, countless times, they wetted the tip of the brush with their tongues so they might get nice, clean numerals on the dials," Warren Tibbs told him. "Some of them had fun with it and decorated their fingers and eyelids. One painted a Cheshire Cat grin on her face to surprise her beau. At night, walking from the factory, they all gave off this lambent glow. They must have looked quite lovely, those girls."

The doctor opened his bag.

"My mother used to have one of those alarm clocks," Warren added. "Isn't that something?"

And so the doctor's treatments began.

It was two months later that Warren Tibbs summoned Dr. Tremblay to his own home. "I have things to show you," he said. "You will be amazed."

The doctor walked the mile and a half out to the Tibbs home half in wonder. Two months and the only contact had been through the physics department secretary, who called weekly and then twice weekly for the professor's prescriptions. That day, Warren Tibbs himself opened the front doors, his shirt sleeves rolled up, his smile wide, and his face flushed and vibrant.

"Dr. Tremblay, I have always wanted to do something significant," Warren Tibbs said. "Many think I already have. They are wrong." He was not wearing any socks or shoes, and the doctor noted that the brightness in his face had an intensity that worried him. "I wanted to make my mark, wanted my life to have meaning," Warren Tibbs continued, his whole body nearly shaking with energy, "and now you have made it possible."

And then Warren Tibbs opened the doors to his study. On the leather-banked walls were ten, twenty, thirty canvases, bright paintings thick with roiling swirls of oil, brilliant vermillion, scarlet, gold, and when the doctor peered closer, he saw within the swirls dainty, flickering images of what appeared to be girl sprites or elves dancing, slipping on the tiniest of feet along the swoop and whorl of each throbbing helix.

Paint spattered all over the floors and curtains and dappled Warren Tibbs's trouser cuffs and, the doctor now noticed, streaked up one of his arms. It was in his hair.

"You do not even know yet," Warren Tibbs said, voice scratchy as if he had recently been screaming. He slapped his head against the light plate on the wall and the entire room fell to darkness.

The doctor was transfixed. The sprites, the elves, they glowed with an unearthly power, a searing green luminescence radiating off every canvas and like nothing he had ever seen before. And yet he had. Long ago, in Marfa, Texas. These glowing monuments to all that is mysterious and unreachable and unknown.

Standing there in the dark, looking at these paintings, the doctor immediately knew their power, and they spoke to him, and it was like the voice from the buried center of his own buried heart. Warren Tibbs turned to him, so close the doctor could smell the rotting of his teeth. He felt Warren's hand take his, and the two men stood for some time.

It was that day, the day of the paintings, their light, that Dr. Tremblay saw what was to occur. Walking out, he saw Warren Tibbs's six-year-old daughter dancing pirouettes on the front lawn, waving one of her father's paint brushes like a magic wand. He knew he must do something.

He decided he would perform a courageous act.

Is the spirit capable of achieving what we in our distress must expect of it? That is what Albert Schweitzer asked, and Dr. Tremblay knew the answer.

"Dr. Feelgood," the government man said with a sneer. "You made Warren Tibbs feel so good he stopped taking his heart medication and died."

"That is not how I see it," he replied.

"You must have noted the strain on his heart."

The doctor did not say anything.

"You stopped his heart, Dr. Tremblay."

"His heart had stopped long ago, young man. I merely stopped the thunder in his head."

The night before the jury's verdict, Dr. Tremblay woke with a start. He realized he had been in the midst of a stunningly vivid dream in which before him passed all his patients, eyes bright and glittering, smiling at him, thanking him, hurling their hands out, unknotting their knotted fists, opening their arms to him. Until the last one appeared. Walter Tibbs, of course, and when he smiled there were no teeth inside, only an orbular glow that hummed, like a tuning fork. But as he moved closer, the doctor saw that Warren's mouth was open not in a smile but in terror. As if the light inside was choking him, swallowing him whole.

Shaking in his bedclothes, huddled on his office couch, and the thought came to him: It happened because I was too greedy for love. It was all I wanted.

"Dr. Tremblay," Mrs. Moses-Pittock pleaded as they led him out of the courtroom after the verdict, "you can't leave us. Who will take care of us? Who will take care of me?"

He touched her netted glove with two shaking fingers, looked into her watery gray eyes. "I trust you understand that our hearts can take us all to dark and ill-timed places."

*James Greer*

**JAMES GREER** is the author of two novels: *The Failure* (Akashic, 2010); and *Artificial Light* (Little House on the Bowery/Akashic, 2006), which won a California Book Award for Best Debut Novel. He is also the author of the nonfiction book *Guided By Voices: A Brief History* (BlackCat/Grove, 2005), a biography about a band for which he once played bass guitar.

# the speed of things
## by james greer

### part 1: ego in arcadia

**N**othing would make me happier than to tell you, up front, that everything works out fine in the end. Can't do that, I'm afraid. Not because things don't work out fine in the end, but because I don't know how the end ends. The end hasn't happened yet (as far as I can tell). The end may never happen. Things are moving so quickly these days that the end may come and go and I might not notice. Have to allow for that possibility. Have to allow for every possibility. Facts are engrams. Engrams are hypothetical. Thus: Every. Possible. Outcome.

As for the body lying on the floor a few feet away from where I sit, at my desk: I can talk about that. I can give you a definitive answer with respect to the body. Yes, the blood pooling near her head and, less obviously, the little splatters on and around her bare feet: aftereffects of her transition from life to death by means of a series of bullets discharged from a handgun at close range. I should probably make this much (all right, fine) clear: I did not shoot the gun. She didn't shoot the gun. I have no idea who shot the gun. Not sure it matters. The gun got shot, right? A shot gun is not necessarily a shotgun, would be one conclusion you could draw from the

Cannot let this incident interfere with my work schedule. I am extremely busy. I'm on seven different deadlines. Which when you think about it, as I am sometimes given to do (think about it), presents a sort of ironie du sort. (Now I'm just playing word games.) But serious. The line drawn outside a prison beyond which prisoners were liable to be shot. From that idea to this: how? Is there any sense in which missing a deadline corresponds to going further than allowed and therefore liable to be shot and killed? Perhaps going further than allowed, yes, that much one can grant, but everything after therefore is a damned lie.

En attendant, everything is killing me. Not just the seven different deadlines but the expectations. People who know me, who have made the mistake of not shutting up (for good) the minute we met, have a series of expectations that seem to grow, perversely, in accord with my ability to disappoint each and every one. You have to say "each and every" in that sentence for the rhythm, not the meaning. The meaning can go to hell, along with all the people who expect things from me. I know my limits. I know when I've reached my limits. Hey, guess what? I've reached my limits. I might be, well, actually I am, let's not kid ourselves, he said, of at least superhuman intelligence and—did you see that? Her arm just twitched. That was disconcerting—supernal intuition, but even such a one has limits. I see everything, I understand everything, and this happens at both the conscious and all twelve subconscious levels simultaneously. You'd reasonably expect a man with such abilities to be sotted with power, joy-drunk, unintimidated by intimations of mortality. To some extent that is actual factual. To some extent just silly. I have to draw the. It's a question of. Guess. Guess not. Huh.

In the motion picture *Meet John Doe* starring that one guy and that girl and directed by what's-his-name (1939), movement is both created and just happens. Think on this: w/r/t film and music, all forms of dissemination heretofore have involved circular objects, spinning. No matter how far back you looky-loo. Revolvers each and every one, but no more, no more, no more, no more. I don't "these days" know the shape of the medium. Does anyone? Is there a shape? I have seen certain media represented as a waveform, but I suspect that waveform is merely a visual translation of a shapeless batch of numbers. Thing I need to know, has art become math or has math become art, (and) is there a meaningful distinction?

A John Doe club forms for the purpose of improving relations between and among neighbors. That's all. To be a better neighbor. Not really sure how such a thing, even if fueled by a despicable despot, takes root and flowers. Where I live, there are only seven or ten people grouped in ten or seven tin houses, then nothing interesting for many kilometers. An island afloat in the middle of a great city. Everyone is related either by marriage or blood, and everyone keeps to himself. Family members do not talk to family members. No one talks to anyone. Where I live is spectral silent except for noises made by elements and animals. Where I live is nowhere.

The potential when you harness the separate units of a great number of John Doe clubs toward some end other than neighborly. In and out of doors. Well, that's just frightening. If you agree raise your hand. No, other hand. Theoretically I am writing a history of the Federal Reserve Bank. I say theoretically because I don't believe the Federal Reserve Bank exists, evidence to the contrary notwithstanding. You could, I suppose, say with some accuracy that I'm writing a history of nothing. The History of Nothing. Written in Nowhere. Written By. (Hope is in the hand that hits you.)

I have been contracted. Contacted? After a while you forget the smaller differences. This is a known side effect, according to the materials accompanying my prescription of PROVIGIL. I thank, I praise, I grant every, no, each and every day. One hundred milligrams in the morning is my prescriptive dose. I'm not good at following instructions. Too proud or something. Nine is the number of the muses, so nine hundred milligrams in the morning suits my symmetry. Many people say: *Where would I be without coffee?* and for coffee you can substitute other stimulants or depressants or ampersands. But where would I be without coffee? Added to nine muses of PROVIGIL you can accomplish worlds. You can eliminate sleep from your diet. How super, my love!

$C_{15}H_{15}NO_2S$

Walking through tall pines, trunks pasted with greeny moss, forest floor covered in a mass of needles and cones and deciduous leaves, brown or yellow according to their last request, Aunt Panne was over-brimmed with holy spirit of trees. Praying as she walked, slowly, for soul of dead girl lying on the floor next to desk of Writer. Dead girl or possibly not-dead girl, id est dying girl. Lovely deep blue of her lips.

Mossy ruins of a water mill. Heavyset old man with dropsical jowls and comically large glasses sat on a rotting tree limb chewing a reed.

"I am Aunt Panne."

"I am Paul Volcker, twelfth chairman of the Federal Reserve, 1979–1987. I grew up in Teaneck, New Jersey."

"What brings you to the forest, Paul Volcker?"

"I'm waiting for Writer to remember me."

"There's a plaque here by the ruin of the millstone. I can't read it."

"Because it's in Gallic. The gist of the inscription is that these ruins are symbolic of a larger wreck."

"Well, that makes sense. Did you know the dead or dying girl?"

"Not personally. Only what you read in papers. When there used to be papers. Newspapers, I mean. Les journaux."

"It wasn't all that long ago."

"No, it wasn't. You're right."

"By larger wreck you mean the design?"

"Yes."

"I've been wondering lately if the seeming incoherence of the design isn't contained, somehow, within an even larger design whose outlines we can't see. And that maybe this imperceptible scheme makes perfect sense."

"I don't engage with poetry." Paul Volcker stopped chewing his reed and fished in his jacket pocket for a small notebook.

"*Meet John Doe*," he read aloud from the notebook.

"And then what?" asked Aunt Panne.

"That's all I have so far."

"It's a good start."

Aunt Panne left Paul Volcker sitting by the remains of the mill and continued through the forest, following a path that was no path. She knew that Paul Volcker was worried about the farmers driving their tractors down C Street NW to blockade the Eccles Building, but he would never admit it, not to her, anyway. Maybe he wouldn't admit it to anyone, anymore. Maybe the reason he wouldn't admit it is related to the reason he was sitting on the rotting tree limb by the old water mill.

Was there even a trace of whatever water source once drove the mill? As she moved farther and farther away, Aunt Panne's memory similarly receded. She could no longer picture Paul Volcker's face. She could no longer in any detail picture the mossy ruin of the mill. It was entirely possible, she admitted to herself as she trudged up a gentle slope slick with mud from a recent rain, that she had imagined the whole interval. The words *lacuna* and *caesura* flitted through her brain, for a moment, and then disappeared.

Okay, but if you allow one example do you have to allow them all? Do you admit the unreality of experience generally if one experience turns out to be illusion? The brain is capable of many things when its circuits are working, even more when overloaded with catecholamines and hypothalamic histamines. The synaptic terminals release these oracles into the floodstream and you start to see things: Is it the future? Is it the past? Is it a kind of present that would otherwise be invisible to our seven dulled senses? Or is it, as most would have you think, a fantasy, the product of a disordered mind. Consciousness infected with chemicals, perception out of step with consensus. When you apply reason to the problem, you kill the problem. You derive a solution. Aunt Panne mistrusted solutions. She would rather beggar the question by withholding logic, and thus arrive at the edge of the forest rather than, say, a small clearing or a mossy ruin.

Approaching the ecotone she could see cows grazing in the meadow.

## part 2: rule bretagne

Snow came in bunches to Bon Repos, on the border of the Forêt de Quénécan. The companions of the abbey were put to work sweeping the courtyard early on the morning of December 19 in the Year of Our Lord. The blinking lights of the snowplows had moved far enough away from the courtyard that you could no longer hear the susurrus of their heavy tires, nor the scrape of metal against. This has been the coldest winter of our lives. In the memory of our lives. There has been a record chute of snow. The cars are corked for miles, and hours, on the autoroutes. On the radio you are warned to bring a thermos of some hot liquid and *"perhaps something to eat"* before you set out in your car. What kind of a person would set out in his car under such perturburant circumstances? What kind of person says "set out in his car"? The wrecked bulkheads massed along the shore, covered in fresh snow, no longer move, but boy they sure do work. How do you cut the GPS tag from under your skin? You use a stolen knife. You ask the girl to use the knife because you can't do it yourself. That's how the girl ended up dead, on your floor, in your room, because she removed the GPS tag. It's starting to come back now, but in fragments. In packets.

Everybody's got a past. Everybody stinks of time. But the photography is so pure that you don't mind. The rhythm of the shots, and the rhythm within the shots, matches with exquisite rigor the languid movements of the actors inside the frame. Only the music jars. The music is ridiculous, overstated, too much. "Tonight the gates of Mercy will open." That's what the music wants to say. The clarinets. I see a crowd of black hats, everyone playing the clarinet. There's nothing wrong with the clarinet in principle. With any woodwind.

New rule: no one speaks. Not for any reason. Words have only ever caused problems. I can think of no exceptions. Everything will be communicated in images, only. No intertitles, subtitles, supertitles, titles, title cards. The moving image versus the static (photo) is obviously superior. An image that moves offers a more complete set of the infinite fractions of solitude, according to N. The history of cinema is the history of the image. Without words. The paradox of using words to describe things that. Text is text is text. This is not a text. In the event of an actual text, you would have been directed by the appropriate emergency services to destroy all evidence of yourself. I do not feel pain. Thunder and lightning ask my approval. What some call prayer is easily misused, but I command the seas.

I have no reason to doubt. I have no reason to believe. I got no reason, I prefer no reason at all. Crows gather on every street corner. Talking about something I can't quite. What's the point of so many crows? Crown, crow, cow. Unusually, you can do that in Russian too.

Phil Esposito was the consensus pick in the living room for the trivia question, *Which Buckthorn had been the fastest to score fifty goals in one season?* Writer didn't wait to hear the answer. If not Esposito, who? Cashman? Bucyk? What difference does it make? They were all fucking great. Ten seconds later his father actually said, "I have seen some terrible calls in my life, but that one takes the cake," concerning a potentially dodgy hooking call on Buckthorn player Sad Strawbo. The answer to a more pertinent question was soon thereafter provided by Sabater Pi and his caliginous table of incantatory engrams. Without the help of Sabater Pi, one finds it unlikely that anything would ever get done by anyone. A study of helicopter pilots suggested that 600 milligrams of PROVIGIL given in three doses can be used to keep pilots alert and maintain their accuracy at predeprivation levels for forty hours without sleep. Another study of fighter pilots showed that PROVIGIL given in three divided 100-milligram doses sustained the flight-control accuracy of sleep-deprived F-117 pilots to within about twenty-seven percent of baseline levels for thirty-seven hours, without any considerable side effects.

The exact mechanism of action of PROVIGIL is unclear, although numerous studies have shown it to increase the levels of various monoamines, namely: dopamine in the striatum and nucleus accumbens; noradrenaline in the hypothalamus and ventrolateral preoptic nucleus; and serotonin in the amygdala and frontal cortex. While the coadministration of a dopamine antagonist is known to decrease the stimulant effect of amphetamine, it does not entirely negate the wakefulness-promoting actions of PROVIGIL. This is not by any means the whole story.

Sabater Pi stands over his engrams and mutters incantations. These incantations are the stuff of ice creams, through which the world learns its manners. Without Sabater Pi's engrams, the world would have no memory. He decides which to keep and which to discard. It's a very important job. It might be the only important job. Sabater Pi had just decided that the engram of the dead girl in Writer's room must at all costs be kept. Could not for any reason be removed. He walked to a corner of his office, sat down at a comically small desk, and began typing.

Writer was startled by the sudden whir and clunk of the fax machine on the floor by his feet. He remembered that the Icelandic magician Flute Guðmundsdottir had once told him that her magic was meant to represent or emulate the sound of the modern world, its electronic machinery in constant motion, humming and buzzing and belling in the background even when no one was listening. This had never made any sense to Writer. He had tried to discuss the issue with Bragi Ólafsson, an Icelandic novelist who had once helped out in Sykurmolarnir, which was the name of a circus act in which Flute had also participated, doing—something. But Writer's attempt to reach Ólafsson through his American publisher had been unsuccessful, and so with some reluctance he had dropped the matter. Throughout his conversation with Flute, she had licked her lips repeatedly, small pink tongue darting out of her mouth to moisten this or that small section of unglossed upper or lower lip. It was a reflexive action. She wasn't aware she was doing that, he remembered thinking. But also a familiar one. People who are nervous, or who take any form of stimulant, even coffee, are prone to this reflex. The stimulant produces a sensation of dryness in the mouth and lips that no amount of water can remedy. There would be no reason, Writer reasoned, for Flute to be nervous in his company, in room 59 of the Chateau Marmont in Los Angeles, California. She was drinking from a deep glass of still water. It was exactly noon o'clock.

The sound of the modern world scared the wits right out of Writer (whose real name was Thomas Early). The sound of the modern world was linked inextricably to the speed of the modern world. The latter was very, very fast, and getting faster. At—what's the usual phrase—an "exponential rate." One moment we're all prosperous and happy, seals basking on the warm rocks of midday sun off the coast of Maine in summer. The next we're falling, endlessly, down a hole that used to be a floor but is no longer a floor. The banking system had run out of money, as Thomas Early understood the situation, and so everyone had run out of money, and even though everyone had run out of money years and years ago, for some reason this now actually mattered. Hence the panicky tumble down the black hole of the future, end over end, bottom over top, will-ye nill-ye, and God help us if we ever reach any kind of definite denouement, because a back-of-the-envelope calculation indicates that an abrupt halt would result in a gelatinous mess.

The best we can hope for, then, in the current situation, is to keep falling. Even though it seems as if we're falling faster and faster, we're actually falling at the same speed. The speed of a falling object does not depend on its mass. That you are a (much) fatter person than me does not mean you will fall faster. We all started at the same height, from the same point, and Galileo has proved that we will all be crushed to death simultaneously.

We are aware of our many misdeeds, our failings, our weaknesses, our fears, our shame. We do not know how to exculpate ourselves. (Having no religion to rely on.) We do not know whether to exculpate ourselves, having no moral or philosophical base from which to extrude the principle of sin. Because we were brought up short. We were all brought up short in a long, tall world.

The dead girl's mistake was indulging her appetite for existence. We all make the same mistake, and the mistake is always fatal. An eighty-three-year-old woman is in a coma after having been attacked at the Mairie de Clichy métro station by a fourteen-year-old Romanian kid. A former journalist was killed by his seventeen-year-old son because the son was unhappy with the five hundred euros per month his father was giving him as an allowance. A man found two thousand euros, cash, in the street. He turned it over to the police. A judge ruled that the two thousand euros does not belong to the man, and is instead being kept by the court until the real owner of the money can be determined. The man declared himself in an interview to be "disappointed" by the court's ruling. "Honesty doesn't pay," he said.

Potter's Field ain't such a faraway stare when you've one foot in the quick. An argument between scholars, already tenuous, becomes untenably ephemeral within minutes if you put it in (a cloud). Unsearchable, unfindable, irretrievable. Lost. The most common side effect of speed is the acceleration of loss.

The fax from Sabater Pi was very short. It read, in full: *The dead or dying girl is you.*

William T. Vollmann

**WILLIAM T. VOLLMANN** is the author of twenty books, including *Europe Central*, winner of the National Book Award; *Riding Toward Everywhere*, an examination of the train-hopping hobo lifestyle; and *Imperial*, a panoramic look at one of the poorest areas in America. He has also won the Whiting Writers' Award, the PEN Center USA Literary Award for Fiction, a Shiva Naipaul Memorial Prize, and the Strauss Living Award from the American Academy of Arts and Letters. His journalism and fiction have been published in the *New Yorker*, *Esquire*, *Spin*, and *Granta*. Vollmann lives in Sacramento, California.

# no matter how beautifully it stings
## by william t. vollmann

*Note to the Reader: The following passages have to do with speedy substances, which, like any loyal American, I know only in the most theoretical sense. —WTV*

Her face was already smoother when he looked in the mirror. He thought it was the estrogen but Rosa said it was only autosuggestion. (He had a dream that he was walking with Rosa and everyone humiliated him; Rosa said it was because they could see, thanks to the crimson collar of the sweater he wore beneath his jacket, that he was a woman.) Often now he felt as lovely-pure as this transparent meth crystal now partially crumbled to glassy sand within the multiple-folded scrap of newspaper. He broke it in half. He inhaled. The septum of his nose ached. His nostrils watered. Then he began to feel the happy lively feeling; he was alive again, "in the moment" as we Californians say. His nipples itched.

Do you want any, darling?

No, thank you, said Rosa, doing her mascara.

His penis hardened delightfully. He saw everything better; he could practically count the revolutions of the fan blades on the ceiling; oh, he surely could have had he wanted to.

While Rosa glossed her lips, he had another sniff.

Rosa offered to do his makeup, but tonight he did not care to honor his inner feminine in any outer way; better to remain a double agent. So while Rosa combed out her Isabel wig he laid happily spreadeagled on the bed, with another shot of whiskey in his hand, playing with the gray hairs on his nipples, his penis hard like never before.

One was supposed to leave the room key at the office, but he put it in his pocket. They went downstairs to the rental car. Rosa was the driver and he the navigator. It was just dusk as they rolled out of Santa Monica past the motels on Ocean and the cool beads of traffic. The sting of crystal was delicious in his nostrils. It was going to keep him excited for all of the thousand miles down Santa Monica Boulevard to the Western girls and the blond California girls with net purses. His powers of perception may safely be defined as godlike, although I grant that later he could not always remember his observations. In traffic behind taxis he saw into every car, reading the emotions of all parties even when only the backs of their heads offered themselves to his discernment. As for Dolores, she spotted a man on a bench; she could have counted every hair on his hands. Two couples crossed the street, and to her this was unique and even important. A man and a woman were kissing. Dolores got hot, and slid her big hand up Rosa's skirt. But then as they crossed Fourth he was enraged rather than titillated to find a man put his hand on a brunette's hips when *he* wanted to do it. Then the illuminated freeway became an intergalactic ride, and these were the constellations:

**PSYCHIC READING BY EVE**
Del's Saloon
OPEN LATE
**Colby Avenue**
*Feminine Touch Makeovers*
**LEGEND OF THE SEEKER**
**Dolores Restaurant**

and the 405 freeway where the world was darkened by red lights. Rosa seemed a trifle disappointed in him, so he put on lipstick.

SMOKING DEATHS THIS YEAR
*Afrodita Flowers*
**Selby Avenue**

(the meth shining loyally in his being, the lights calm)

**LOS ANGELES – TEMPLE**
*Casa Isabel Wedding Gowns*
Come Unto Me Katholic Shoppe
Gentlemen's Club
*PROSTHETIC HEAVEN*
GRANITE MONUMENTS
EYES BY HANNA
**Hair by Rosa**
Dr. S. R. Yemadjian, Fashion—Liposuctions
A. A. Liquors
**A. A. A. Deli & Liquor**
AAAAH! Female Rejuvenation
Little Friends Preschool
*Little Sweeties Massage*
**BIG JOHN'S MARITAL AIDS**
**Ron's Kickass Butt Burgers**
*CARNICERIA — DIVORCE*
**Dignity Plus Discount Cremations**
Esmerelda's Lingerie
Hollywood Wonder Caverns
**Grinning Cave Virtual Thrill Adventures**

**Young Forever Breast Reduction**
Buy One, Get One Free
**Avenue of the Stars**

and high dark towers whose rectangular windows were usually yellow but sometimes silver gathered them in like the arms of a harbor or moonbase, the red blear of the Beverly Hilton promising them that their night could be as dirty, fun, or sinister as they cared to make it; and then it grew extremely dark on Wilshire Boulevard. This long grayish-white rectangular building over there against the dirty dark cubes, what would that have meant to anyone whose gaze had not been so enhanced by meth? And what did it mean? *He* knew, but what he knew he never told me, so I cannot put it into this book. His eyesight was getting keener by the instant. His best friend Luke used to have 20-10 vision, although now that was going away. Now he understood what it must have been like for Luke, this confidence and competence; and already they were crossing Rodeo Drive. Los Angeles was flat and white and cool.

He experienced a glowing feeling, deviled warm and deviled dark, but no, neither dark nor cool—perfectly at ease, with a faintly bitter taste in his mouth, his lipstick greasy—

**CITY OF WEST HOLLYWOOD**
**Almost Everyday People**
Tell Us Your Story
*BEST BURGER IN TOWN*
Movie Star Styling Palace
Ereshkigal Middle Eastern Delights
TANGO GRILL

(not to mention the glowing massage parlor on La Cienega,

then Love Connection, Love Correction, Tasty Donuts, Crescent Heights Boulevard, Hollywood Electric Vacuum and Sewing, Paris House Nude Adults Only, Fat Burger—and then the velvet grid)

## La Brea Avenue
## $1 CHINESE EXPRESS
Adult Books
CALIFORNIA SURPLUS MART
El Centro Mini Mart
TRANS MAGIC
Gold Diggers Entertainment

—and on Western a police car screamed by—

## Tropical Fish and Birds
## DR. SKIN

I want to go to Dr. Skin, he thought; but what if he's creepy, and instead of improving my skin into womanly smoothness he skins me alive or turns me into a tattooed mummy?

They parked and went to a bar which had been recommended by an expert drinker named Mr. Joseph Mattson. It was called the Black Hole, and indeed it was a narrow, lightless place, deserving of the dark fumigation recommended by the fifteenth-century *Book of Buried Pearls* for those who wish to find the invisible pathway beneath the white mountain north of the Great Pyramid of Giza; here refined gold awaits the seeker who has escaped Dr. Skin. The little Japanese barmaid wore bigger breasts than Dolores. On the hot black stinking sticky walls, dancing girls had been painted in phosphorescently artificial hues. They could have been ancient terra-cotta Sirens from whose flesh the

222 CR THE SPEED CHRONICLES

pigment was flaking. The black picnic tables were empty, but four men sat drinking quietly at the bar. It was almost Halloween. He sat down beside Rosa, gazing at a plastic jack-o'-lantern while they drank beer in plastic cups. Rosa laughingly said: I wonder why it is that the toilet seat is always up in the women's room? Around midnight the T-girls began to swish in; he especially liked the long-haired girl in the snappy dress shaking her hair, acned rough face. On the black man's lap, the white legs of two capering girls opened and closed, speaking to him like lips whose tongues were hiding. There was a curtain like a pair of nylon stockings, and it kept wavering and the busiest T-girl kept wavering through it in and out of the street, from which came another T-girl in a black skirt who took her by the hand and they went into the ladies' room. Not all of them were tall; some little young ones reminded him of black ducks swimming and pecking in the green water. There was a woman whose eyes were so white in the darkness; Rosa also loved her, so that when they gazed at her together his heart became as blue and pure as her eyeliner. Rosa, seeing how shy he felt, rose and entered this woman's golden screaming glow; she whispered into her ear, and the woman smiled, at which he began to glow at once, staring into her eyes. The woman accepted Rosa's hand. They approached him.

What's your name? she asked him.

Dolores, he replied. And yours?

Luz María Salcido.

Do you like the Black Hole?

Better than picking grapes all day in Coachella.

Soon they were in the woman's apartment, playing with her cosmetics.

Just as a line or two of meth on the second day, no matter how beautifully it stings the nasal passages or even how well one has just slept, is never as thrillingly joyous as on the first—nasal secretions run down into the throat, bitter rather than salty; and the feeling with which one is presently gifted is no high, merely a sort of weary steadfastness, as if consciousness has squared its shoulders; then slowly, slowly, one comes to feel a trifle better, more wide awake, but impurely so, lacking well being—so Dolores, who had now become a woman to the best of her capabilities, now began to take herself for granted, feeling sometimes almost bored with her lips, anus, and nipples: I'm a woman, and who cares? Do I particularly care about my down-stairs neighbor Adelina? Are whatever pieties her wrinkled old brain produces any more or less of a miracle than the fact that between her legs rides a dried-up gray-haired slit? Who am I to be impressed by her, myself, or anything? What I live is merely life, nothing better. Anyway, I don't dislike Adelina; I'm even fond of myself; my life is quite fine in that way. What do I wish for? Is nothing better than sexual ecstasy, or self-love, or the love of others? Is boredom my failure or simply a requirement for not dying? I'm *sweating* with boredom! I don't feel good. I must be getting old; I'm hot and achy. No, it must be the hormones, or perhaps some disease.

By degrees her customers had become peculiarly ungrateful, even insulting at times. But then she discovered something nearly as good as Concentrax, and possibly even better. They called it *the green angel*. It was a little pill, you see, a darling little pill, and whenever she took two, or at most three, then no matter whom she was with and whatever she did, she screamingly enjoyed herself. Sometimes *the green angel* even focused her mind so that she could remember any number of ways of being a woman, for instance a certain young girl, so shy, a whispering face-averter, who in the time when Dolores was still a man would gallop upon

his face so freely, and just before she came would always whisper
*fuck!*

A man was sodomizing Dolores, and she loved it. Oh, how
she loved it with the deep joy and purity of desire fulfilled, the
animal present triumphing over the deathly future . . . Wiggling
her bottom for him, leaning on her elbows, she covered her eyes
with both hands as if she felt extremely reserved, then suddenly
drew her hands away, wiggled her bottom as rapidly as she could,
and whispered *fuck!* The man was enchanted.

But soon afterward her big male hands began stinking of
sweat; her aging face went red and ugly; she felt as if contami-
nated liquefied fat were oozing out of the bags under her eyes,
her febrile forehead salty wet, her tongue and glottis tasting like
metal. She blew her nose, and there were flecks of blood in the
mucus. She grew more hot and nauseous by the instant. These
unpleasant sensations seemed to have come from nowhere, but
don't they always? When she lay down, the granules of the pop-
corn ceiling refused to stop enlarging themselves. She closed her
eyes, but her eyelids hurt her aching eyeballs, which sweated and
sweltered in that too-hot darkness. Her face seemed to feel better
when she locked it into a grimace. Why was that? She couldn't
think. When would this go away? It was the third day since she
had last inhaled a line of crystal. The sweat on the backs of her
hands and between her fingers afflicted her almost intolerably.
It felt gummy and corrosive at the same time. She wished to lie
perfectly still on her back in a cool dim room. With considerable fortitude she managed to take a shower. Then she put on
a clean loose dress and lay down. Instantly she could smell the
stench of her armpits, which she had cleaned many times with
a bar of stinging soap. The sweat on her upper lip stung almost
intolerably. Sores broke out on her tongue. Twin crescent zones
of hideous sweat erupted beneath her eyebrows, whose fine, al-

most imperceptible hairs exuded foulness. Her heart was beating very rapidly. The hairs on the backs of her arms began to sting. In her breastbone, a wide hot oval of tenderness now manifested itself, not entirely unpleasantly. Dolores lay as motionless as she could, waiting for these symptoms to pass. Now it was the backs of her wrists which felt the hottest and wettest. The insides of her elbows stung numbly. Her dress clung to her flesh like the burning poison shirt of Nessus. Her back ached. Each bone within her fingers threatened to shatter. She wanted to wipe away the sweat on her upper lip, but feared that the side of her hand might adhere there. She would have used yesterday's panties, which lay on the floor beside her, but although she could see them, she could not reach them. How hot it was here, how impure! She could not escape from feculence.

The next day the withdrawal afflicted her only in throbbing nauseating wavelets, and the day after that she was perfect. Now she knew how to manage crystal: once a week would be best. For the other times there were Concentraxes, powder-trains of cocaine snuffed up through twenty-peso bills, crack rocks, tequila, beer, whiskey, and, of course, *the green angel*. The trick was to parcel out these various vitamins and staples, so that no single one could bite too deep. When all else failed, and certainly when anything succeeded, there remained orgasm itself.

Thanks to this superbly practical insight, Dolores soon found herself quite rich in pleasures and hours. All day she rested or played with herself; all night, so it seemed, she expressed her womanhood by taking in the penises of this world, whose friends, clients, and encounters all became stacked up upon each other. Sometimes she wondered whether this was what she had made all her prior sacrifices for, but the sensations of the Femerol still thrilled her sometimes in her spectacular nipples, *the green angel* was good to her, and many of her sexual encounters gave her great joy. She said goodbye to this man and that; sometimes she wished to find a woman to love and live with forever as she should have done with Rosa, but how could she expect to see anyone like Rosa again? In a lesbian bar in Tijuana the women had been far from kind to her, and in Xalapa there might be no such place; not even Ana María had known of one. So happily Dolores let herself be carried down the weeks and months. Surely there would come another purpose, or at least a new adventure. Descending the stairs to greet her neighbor Adelina, she smiled at the world, smoothed her hair, straightened her dress, and hurried off to buy just a little more crystal. She was already itching to get her sweet breasts sucked.